The Hated Billionaire

Erica Frost

Published by Erica Frost, 2023.

THE HATED BILLIONAIRE

First edition. May 6, 2023.

Copyright © 2023 Erica Frost.

ISBN: 979-8223966852

Written by Erica Frost.

Table of Contents

Chapter 1: Christina..1

Chapter 2: Brett..5

Chapter 3: Christina..11

Chapter 4: Christina..17

Chapter 5: Christina..24

Chapter 6: Brett..30

Chapter 7: Brett..35

Chapter 8: Christina..45

Chapter 9: Christina..53

Chapter 10: Christina...56

Chapter 11: Christina...64

Chapter 12: Christina...68

Chapter 13: Brett...76

Chapter 14: Christina...82

Chapter 15: Christina...89

Chapter16: Brett..92

Chapter 17: Christina...98

Chapter 18: Brett.. 106

Chapter 19: Christina.. 110

Chapter 20: Brett.. 116

Chapter 21: Christina.. 123

Chapter 22: Brett.. 127

Chapter 23: Christina.. 133

Chapter 24: Brett.. 137

Chapter 25: Christina.. 141

Chapter 26: Christina.. 148

Epilogue: 155

The Hated Billionaire
Bad Boy Enemies To Lovers Billionaire
Romance

By: Erica Frost

Foreword

I hate my boss. But he is so damn sexy.

I met Brett Caden when I started at Caden Global, five years ago. My first impression wasn't good – sexy, but a real jerk. A smooth, conceited jackass. Or so I thought. I was so excited when I finally made it to a senior exec position, but the one bad thing was I had to see Caden every other day. I thought that was a hardship, until one night when I had to work late.

The last person I would have expected help from was Caden. But, weirdly enough, he did help me. I also didn't expect myself to end up in his arms, but that happened too. Now I just don't know how I am going to hide all my secrets from him.

The Hated Billionaire

Chapter 1: Christina

"Hey! Christina!" someone called. I turned around to look who it was, my long hair bouncing on my shoulders. I had meant to put it up today. I pushed it out of my eyes. I spotted my colleague, standing at her desk. She was waving a form at me.

"Hey." I walked back. I squinted at the form. I probably should get my eyes checked, but I know myself – I'd never do the glasses thing. I was told once that my hazel eyes were my best feature, and I'm sticking with that. I frowned at her.

"It's that form you wanted me to check through. All done. You can just sign it and we'll send it off. Looks good to me."

"Thanks, Neela," I said. I passed it to her and then she passed it back to me.

"Distracted?"

I laughed. "Yeah. Kind of. I have a meeting with the dragon in about fifteen minutes."

"Oh. A dragon, is he?"

"No, not really," I said. "Dragons are too nice."

We both laughed. She knows me well. She also knows I hate our boss.

I took the form, headed up the hallway and then went left, into the boardroom.

I was early.

I felt a sigh of relief wash through me. I still had a few minutes to prepare. I went to the window, checking my reflection. I had a long face with high cheekbones, and most of my friends told me I was good looking. I wiped off a smudge of lipstick carefully. I had chosen dark pink today – I remember a friend telling me it enhanced my eye-color. I tucked chocolate-brown hair behind my ears and carefully brushed some smeared blush in place.

It mattered, to look nice. Not that I cared what Mr. Caden thought of me – not exactly. I just didn't want him to think badly of me.

I checked the room. Was the projector ready to project from the notebook? I went to check. Dax, who usually checks the cables, always forgets to turn the projector on. I checked. It was on.

"Great."

I was just moving from the speaker's place when someone came in through the door.

"Are you speaking today, Ms. Bradfield?" Mr. Caden asked.

"No," I said hastily. "No, I'm not. That's Ted, and he's not here."

"Yes. I can see that."

I blushed. Did he have to be so rude? He raised a brow at me, unsmiling. I couldn't help noticing, even as I remembered anew that he was a jerk, how good-looking he unfortunately was.

With a thin face, high cheekbones and dark hair, he had a great deal in the looks drawer already. Added to that, he had hooded green eyes. Honestly, did he really have to be so stunning? He walked past me to the front of the table and even as I wanted to smack him for pushing me out of the way, I also couldn't help but notice that he moved beautifully.

"So, Miss. You are taking notes?" he asked me.

"Yes," I said. I felt annoyed again. Just because I happened to be the only other woman who was at the meeting, besides one colleague, didn't mean I was automatically the team-secretary. I was the senior marketing executive. He ought to know that – he was one of the people who got me promoted.

I scowled up at him.

He smiled, thinly. I felt my blood race. How dare he? He always acted as if my annoyance was solely to gain his attention. Which made it all the harder to be around him. The more annoyed I got, the more he seemed to get amused.

I shifted in my seat. It was silent in there. No people talking to distract us, no fan, no keyboard. Just me and him and the sound of breathing.

He looked up from the keys.

"The cable's not connecting."

"What?" I frowned. I'd just checked them.

I stood up, high-heels clicking on the floor. We had a really nice floor in the boardroom. It was a really nice room, too, in an old-fashioned way. I just wished that I wasn't stuck in it alone with Mr. Annoying. I let out a deep breath and looked at the laptop.

"The cable's not working. Look." He pointed. I could see that there was an error message. I ran a hand through my hair. I could smell him, this close. Cologne and spice. I felt my body ache. Why did somebody so annoying have to be so sexy?

I breathed slowly. I tried to think of a solution.

"Yes, the cable's not working. Pull it out and rub the end on a hanky or something. It's probably static."

He looked at me. I hate it when I do that sometimes. I can't help telling people what to do. I guess it's one of the reasons why I am in the job I'm in, but I could see on his face that he'd not expected it. I took a deep breath.

"Why would I do that?" He was looking at me, and I didn't know how to interpret his expression. I raised one eyebrow.

"Because the connector's static," I said. "Wiping it with something discharges it. Here." I wiped it.

"Thank you," he said.

"Now try it," I said. I was surprised that my voice was tight. What was wrong with me? I looked up at him. "If you connect it now, maybe the projector will recognize it."

"Great," he said. He put the connector in.

It worked.

He looked at me, surprised. I wanted to smile, but I kept my face neutral. I wasn't about to put aside my dislike and smile at him. I felt triumphant, since I was fairly sure he had low expectations of my fixing anything. I was saved from needing to say anything as the rest of the executive team came in, walking briskly. I looked up at Brett Caden, but he was uploading the presentations.

I bent over and tried hard to concentrate properly.

Chapter 2: Brett

I looked at the woman who was sitting down at the boardroom desk. She was angry with me – I could feel her anger practically burning the oxygen around her. I also couldn't help noticing how sexy she looked. She had left her dark hair loose; her profile was elegant and she'd used makeup carefully to enhance her already-considerable beauty. Teamed up with a tight top and jacket, both of which complimented her fine body, I couldn't ignore her.

She was a senior executive and I had been aware of her considerable appeal since promoting her. It was something I'd fought as much as I could, hiding behind my aloofness whenever she was near. It was a good defense, being aloof, even though this employee made it very difficult. It was something I'd worked on to try and give me an edge in business. It was usually simple, but with Ms. Bradfield I was stumped – ignoring her was virtually impossible.

"Good morning, everyone," I greeted. "Before I start, I need to thank Ms. Bradfield for fixing the equipment." I gestured to the projector. "She managed to get the projector running when I was a bit stumped, I can admit."

I was surprised when Ms. Bradfield looked at me with a look that might have melted the electronics in the laptop, if it had been in the way. Her anger was intensified by my innocent comment. And somehow, that made her even sexier. I cleared my throat. I did not need to be getting interested in her while standing here.

"Right. Now, with no further delay, we can begin. Ted, I understand you have some information to share with us." I turned to our technical expert. He nodded, clearing his throat and getting ready to begin.

"I have some reports on the new equipment we have planned to purchase overseas," the guy started. I was sitting down at the end of the table, trying to pay attention to the talk. I couldn't help glancing across at Ms. Bradfield every so often. I wished I didn't find her so hot. I wasn't supposed to find the employees attractive.

I had run this company for ten years and I hadn't got there by getting distracted, I told myself. I bent over my iPad, trying to make notes.

I looked up as Ted flipped to a slide, a picture of some new-fangled printing equipment that we were planning to invest in. I had read the specs myself and I didn't really need to watch this part of the presentation, but I felt bad ignoring it. Besides, ignoring the speech meant I had more chance of getting wrapped up in distracting thoughts. Like thoughts about Ms. Bradfield.

I focused on the new high-quality press equipment and tried not to think about the audience too much.

"Um, Ted?" somebody asked, sticking up a hand. I frowned. Normally, I liked employees to wait until a presentation was finished before asking a question, but I ignored it.

"Yeah?" he asked.

"Um...in the slide, you gave the price for refillable cartridges in yen? What is it in dollars?"

"Oh!" Ted reddened. "Yeah. Sorry. Anyone got today's rate?"

I flipped to my phone but someone else got there faster. Somebody noted down the value and we moved to the next topic. I was distracted by somebody dropping a pen and then bending to get it.

Ms. Bradfield was taking notes.

I watched her as she worked, her head bent down over the paper. Her hair was tucked behind an ear and, every so often, stray curls fell into her eye and she reached to tuck them back. I watched her hand as it touched her soft skin and ached to touch it. I wondered how her lips tasted – probably like strawberries, I imagined. In reality, she looked so mad at me every time she sent a glance in my direction that I'd be lucky if I wasn't actually set aflame by an angry look from her.

I grinned to myself. I didn't know what I'd done. Something about me must just offend her. I would try to keep my distance, however much I longed to taste those sweet lips or to undress her beautiful curves.

"Mr. Caden?"

"Um, yes?" I went red, realizing that everyone had stopped talking. Ted was standing at the screen, and to guess from the expectant faces looking at me, I was supposed to say something.

"Mr. Caden? It's your turn to explain the employment plan for the phase-three growth-plan."

"Oh!" I reddened. "Um, yeah. My presentation's uploaded already." I stood and went up to the front. I should have paid more attention to Ted, since the budgeting part of his speech overlapped with mine. As it was, I'd worked out the figures roughly myself while making the plan for the phase, so I knew them without needing to listen to his talk.

"Okay, people," I said, flipping to my first slide, which showed a picture of the company headquarters, here in New York. "So, what we are going to do first of all is launch a strong campaign targeted at attracting graduate employees."

I flipped to the slides my team had prepared, showing our marketing stuff. I have a very strong advertising team – it's distressingly easy to convince people with the right words and pictures. I waited while the team looked over the pictures and then flipped to the next slide.

"We have been talking a lot about printers," I said, flipping to the photos similar to the ones we'd just been viewing. "And of course, for a company like ours, equipment is a key asset."

I could sense Ms. Bradfield watching me. She was taking notes, and her hair was falling into her eye. I fought the urge to stroke it into place. I focused on the presentation. We had worked out a bold scheme of advancement, and I was trying to net a few million in investments to accomplish it, which was why we were here today, brainstorming our presentation to the board.

It was important and I tried hard to focus as I went on with the talk.

"So," I concluded. "With a simple investment of ten million, we can grow the worth of this company tenfold in the next five years." I was really proud of the last chart – it had taken me a week to figure out. I was pleased to see Ms. Bradfield's brow lift. If I could impress her, me and my chart were set to wow the investment-people.

She was looking at me with wide eyes and I felt my body heat up, her admiration making me want her even more.

"Mr. Caden?" someone asked, bringing my mind back to the present. "How are we going to attract new investors?"

"We'll be going to Investcorp investment bank with these numbers. And together with our board, we should be able to net the ten million fairly fast." I explained. I felt confident. The development had all been worked out soundly.

"Yeah, that should work," the questioner agreed, leaving me feeling a little offended. It sure would! I had spent months working on the idea.

"I have a question."

"Yes?" I frowned. Ms. Bradfield almost never raised a hand in meetings. I was puzzled and I waited to hear what she was going to ask.

"In the last figure, I think you have a mistake in one number?"

"Do I?" I was surprised.

"Yeah. I think you put a comma in the wrong place."

"Oh!" I reddened. I really had. I must have worked late and entered it when I was finished. "I'll note that. Thank you." Oddly, having her notice a mistake in my work just made me want to smile.

"It's a pretty nice graph, though. What software is it?" she asked me.

I had to grin. "I was impressed too. It's this really good downloadable software I found. I was thinking I should purchase it for all you guys?" I asked. I was really enjoying talking to her – it made me feel good to have found something that impressed her, and it was great to see her professional interest in the software. She clearly enjoyed her work and I liked that a lot.

"Yeah!" somebody else said, bringing my mind back to where we were. "Imagine what cool projections we could do."

"That would be great," Another said.

"Okay. Let's note it and get onto the next question. I want to get to lunch after we finish."

Laughter. My employees like me. It's what I encourage, though of course I try keep a bit of professional distance. We settled down and moved on to the next inquiry. Then we turned to the actual reason for the meeting – discussing the finer points of what we were presenting to the board – what we had done and what we were going to do next.

It was a good meeting. I was standing at the front of the desk, waiting while the employees filed out, when Ms. Bradfield walked past. She looked up at me. I felt my heart shiver at her being so close.

"Um...Mr. Caden?"

"Please, call me Brett," I said. I usually said that to all my employees once they became senior execs. Most of them still called me Mr. Caden. When I invited her to use my name, it meant something different – at least, it did to me. She raised a brow.

"I wanted to ask you about the software," she said. "I'd really like to be able to use it...Don't forget to send the link to all of us on the emails."

"Yes," I said. "Of course. I look forward to seeing the results when you present your talk for the board next week."

"Of course," she nodded.

I thought her voice sounded almost teasing – but that was probably because that was what I wanted it to sound like. She was standing so close that I could almost feel the warmth of her body and I took a moment to let my eyes wander over her sweet waist and curvy figure.

I watched her walk out, noting the fact that she moved her hips surprisingly sexily as she walked. I forced myself to look down at the laptop, where I was supposed to be saving the presentations and then sorting it out so I could take it back to my room with me. I couldn't help noting the fact that she hadn't called me Brett, and wondering why that was, and whether or not she hated me as much as it seemed.

Chapter 3: Christina

I walked down the hallway towards my office, feeling restless and tired. It was the meeting, I thought – I didn't know why, but somehow it had really got to me: and by "it" I meant Mr. Caden's attitude.

"I hate that man. I hate that man."

I whispered it to myself, standing in the hallway next to the break room. I knew I was just overreacting. I didn't really hate him, of course – I knew those words were a bit strong to express what I felt; but I didn't actually know any other words to express it: if I was honest, I had no idea how I felt.

It was a strong feeling – intense and reactive; one that made me feel oddly discomfited. I felt angry, too, I told myself. That was the only way to describe this strong emotion that coursed through me. It was anger that made me long to annoy him – just anger. I absolutely didn't enjoy his quick responses.

"Had a good meeting?" Neela called as she walked past. I let out my breath in a sigh.

"Not really. I am sick of bosses who think that, just because you're a girl, it's your job to be their personal assistant." That still stung me.

"Hell. That bad?" Neela's beautifully dark eyebrows shot up towards her thick black hair.

"Well, maybe not that bad. I just get sick of people taking it for granted that I'm going to do the minutes. I actually like doing minutes, but that isn't the point. The point is that it isn't a skill based on gender. In my previous position, Jayden kept minutes and it worked really well." I walked back with her towards my office.

Neela grinned. "Well, it's a pity you can't get Jayden up here to take minutes. I would be interested to see how this guy reacted to having a man doing the same job."

"Yeah," I nodded. I would have been curious to see if he took the same patronizing attitude – at very least, it would have been funny to see his face if he asked who was taking the minutes and a big, well-built man put up his hand.

We reached my office and I noticed it was almost time for lunch. I glanced at Neela, who was probably also on her way out. It would be nice to be able to have lunch together – it was rare that we got time to go together, since one or both of us often worked through our break to get stuff done. Maybe today she also had some time for a meal.

As I was about to say something, I was surprised by Mr. Caden. He was coming up the hallway and I felt my heart thump as I looked at him, even as I felt the same strange anger.

"Ms. Bradfield," he said carefully. "I just wanted to say I am about to send the software link to the new mailing list. It is the list called Execs-all, yes?" he inquired, one brow raised.

"Yeah," I said. I wondered why he was asking me. Again, I wasn't the group secretary. Oddly, though, I didn't find myself feeling all that annoyed. I couldn't help noticing that he had a nice smile and that he really did have a stunning body. Yes, he might be a jerk, but he was such a stunning jerk that my blood raced.

"Great. I'll send it over around lunch. Are you on your way out?" he asked.

"Um, yeah," I said, gesturing at Neela, though I hadn't said anything to her sooner.

"Oh," he said. "Great. See you tomorrow for the monthly meeting." He looked a little disappointed.

"Yes," I agreed. I looked after him as he walked away. I felt confused. I would have thought I had been really rude to him – after all, he'd reminded me to call him by his first name, and I'd made a point of avoiding to – but he was acting perfectly normally. Nicer than usual, actually. Weird.

Beside me, Neela chuckled. "What happened to him?" she asked.

"I don't know," I said, feeling my cheeks redden with a blush. "But I don't know what he thinks he's up to. Why should I know which mailing-list to use?" I demanded, cheeks still burning.

Neela grinned. "He should know which mailing-list to use."

"Yeah," I said. I frowned at that. I was sure that he actually did know which mailing-list to use – after all, it was his PA who had set them up and emailed about it in the previous week.

I was still wondering about that as I got my coat and shrugged it on, walking with Neela to the stairs. Had he asked me just to have an excuse to talk to me?

I didn't imagine so.

"Nice coat," Neela commented as we went downstairs. "Where did you get it? I've been meaning to ask you for a while."

"Oh, I saw it in that little store. Near the big mall," I gestured down the street in the downtown direction. "It was on sale and I really liked it, so I bought it." The coat in question was black felt and it really was well-cut and elegant. I felt my cheeks flush with the compliment.

"Well, it looks great," Neela said. "Though you have a different body to me – the waist wouldn't look so good." She gestured at her own figure – she was tall and boyish, where I had more curves.

"Well, you can do that whole loose trousers and loose blouses thing that just looks weird on me," I pointed out. She grinned.

"Everything has its up-side, right?"

We were both laughing as we went out through the front door and turned right, heading towards the restaurant. We always went to the same place, Rothfeld's, if we happened to have time for lunch together.

We walked in and sat down near the back. It was a small café and sandwich-bar, with wood panels on the walls and a really nice faux-Fifties feel. We both loved it in there, with the wood tables and the curtains and weirdly modern crockery, at odds with the retro surroundings.

"The usual?" the waiter asked, spotting us. I nodded.

"Yes, please!"

"Coming right up."

The usual was black coffee, followed by our sandwiches – I always had a grilled vegetable toasted sandwich and Neela always had grilled chicken. We grinned at each other across the table. Neela had taken off her knee-length jacket, and I noticed that she was wearing a smart white shirt underneath, the neck high and buttoned.

"You going to give a presentation later?" I asked as the waiter delivered our coffees. I couldn't imagine why she would be wearing such a formal shirt otherwise – Neela usually dressed in a more Boho way – somewhere between corporate chic and bohemian in a mix that was all her specialty. I added sugar to mine, stirred it and made a face. It was strong! She grinned.

"Yeah. I'm presenting new logo suggestions. Is that strong coffee?" she asked.

"Yes," I said, adding some milk.

"Great. I'm going to need it."

We both laughed. Neela worked with the graphics and advertising part of the company – the graphics team was huge, since they did all the layouts for the magazines as well as doing the branding of the company itself. Neela was also a senior team member and had an amazing creative gift. I always liked looking at her work. I wondered what her presentation would be about.

"I'm doing some promotional stuff for the new extension to the company," she said, when I asked. "It's looking okay. Still not too happy about the colors. I have tried white and green, but I think it's wrong. Just as well it's only a departmental meeting – I don't have to show Mr. Scary there." She gestured towards the building, towards my floor. That meant Brett Caden.

"I don't think I would classify him as scary," I said to myself as much as to her as I sipped my coffee. "More like annoying. He gets on my nerves; that's all."

"Well, I think he's scary," Neela said, then nodded at the waiter as he brought us our sandwiches. "That guy, on the other hand, is rather nice." She looked after the waiter with big eyes.

"Neela!" I chuckled. She grinned. She was seeing a guy in Accountancy and I knew they were very close and happy. She just had a great appreciation for the male body, and always spotted – and commented on – the good-looking men wherever we went, much to my amusement.

"Neela!"

"Well, he is. I can't help seeing." She raised a brow, amused.

I looked after him, but I couldn't help thinking that even though he was probably more built, the waiter had nothing on Mr. Caden.

What the hell? Where did that thought come from? I asked myself.

I was absolutely not interested in Brett Caden. I could see he was good-looking, and I could admit that he was handsome in a smooth, refined way. That was it. I leaned back and took a deep breath and wondered if I was stressed. Maybe the extra work in the last weeks was affecting my thought processes. I couldn't possibly be attracted to my boss. Brett Caden was a jerk.

"What's up?" Neela asked me. She was busy with her salad and she stopped and looked across at me, dark eyes soft.

"Nothing," I said, sipping my coffee and wondering if I should order some water as well. "I just think I've been working a bit hard just lately."

"You think?" Neela chuckled. "Christina, really, you have been working too hard. And I have been as well, now that I am on the topic. So, let's hang out this weekend." She made a wide gesture with one hand. "We haven't done that in ages."

"Sounds good," I said. "What will we do?" I felt my heart lift. It had been ages since we could hang out.

"I don't know," Neela said, taking a sip of her coffee. "I guess we could go shopping and take a walk in the park and maybe give each

other a manicure – not that it'll last until the staff party next month."
She grinned. "You know, that kind of thing. Something that has
absolutely nothing to do with cost or profits or what the hell color
looks good with yellow on an ad."

We both started laughing. I felt myself starting to relax. I probably
had just been working too hard. I needed to give my brain time to get
away from work, like Neela had suggested. A weekend of doing nothing
stressful sounded just perfect. I nodded.

"Sounds great," I said.

"Yeah," she agreed. "And you can help me find an outfit for that
party. For once, someone else can think about what looks good with
yellow."

We both laughed. I felt so glad to have had time to have lunch with
her. I wondered at the fact that I hadn't thought of it sooner. There was
nothing like social time with a friend to help one feel calmer and more
connected – at least, that was what I always found.

We finished lunch and walked back towards the building across the
street. I felt better, and glad to have something to think about that had
absolutely nothing to do with my boss or how annoyed he made me.

Chapter 4: Christina

I woke up early on Saturday, feeling exhausted. That night I had slept badly, waking up with bad dreams. I often had bad dreams when there was noise in the street – as there always was before or during a weekend. It made me feel nervous and restless. I had long ago given up the idea of any sort of therapy, though I knew the nightmares came from the past. I had tried therapy, and found that it didn't agree with me. I had found the therapist inattentive and judgmental.

"Maybe if you find the right person, it'll help," I told myself in the mirror. Some therapists were really good, and actually supported people a great deal, after all.

I pushed the thought away. Maybe one day I would give it another go. For now, I would just hope that a fun day with Neela would be enough to put my worries out of my head.

I went into the shower and washed my hair, enjoying the sensation of the warm water coursing over my body. It felt refreshing and made my sore muscles loosen. I washed my hair and then combed it while it was still wet, giving the style a glance in the mirror.

"Not bad." I smiled at myself, quite pleased with what I saw there.

I have an oval face and I have always taken good care of my skin, meaning that I have a few tiny lines around my eyes at twenty-seven, but no big deal. I combed my thick, dark hair into place – I like it parted a little on one side – and left it to dry, hoping it would bring out the natural wave. I dried off and went through to find something to wear. I planned to wear my new white dress.

"There," I said to myself as I tugged it on and stood in front of my full-length mirror to check the appearance. It was a little casual for the office – thick straps, an A-line and made of a sort of soft, floaty fabric. It had buttons and it was way more informal than anything I usually wore, which was one of the reasons I wanted to wear it – it might help my mind to relax a bit if I wore less-than-formal clothes. I needed to give myself time to think about enjoying myself.

I walked to the kitchen, feeling the fabric of the dress move, light and floating, around my legs. It felt good. It was a warm day and I felt relaxed and ready for an enjoyable weekend.

I looked around my apartment. On the sixth floor, it was beautiful and bright, with big windows and a beautifully-finished interior, mostly a warm beige or cream tone. I had chosen it because of how calming it was – the color-scheme had already been done when I moved in. I appreciate good color-schemes, though I freely admit I am really bad at them.

I heard the doorbell ring just as I was finishing a big bowl of muesli with thick, full-cream yoghurt. I went to answer it, knowing that it must be Neela.

"Hey!" she greeted me, giving me a big hug. She smelled of strawberries and she was wearing a long tunic and wide-legged trousers made out of a light, floaty fabric. "That's a gorgeous dress!"

"Thanks," I said. "I love the color of that tunic! It really looks great on you."

"Thanks," she said with a smile. It was a sort of pale orange, and it matched the trousers, which were a shade of pale brown. Neela had uncannily good skill with color, though she always protested it gave her a headache just to think about it. "So! Have you had breakfast? Shall we go?"

"I was just finished as you walked in," I said, gesturing at the table. I carried the empty bowl and cup to the sink and rinsed them, leaving them on the side-board. I could sort them out later. Neela was looking out through the window, admiring the view.

"It's so relaxing up here," she said, nodding at the window. "It feels like you're so far away from the city. You can just forget about it – basically no traffic."

"Kind of," I said. I could still hear it – especially with the window open. I never slept with the window open if I could avoid it, but last night had been so hot I had done so. I wished I hadn't now – I was still sleepy after a night of restless wakefulness.

"So," Neela asked, giving me a smile. She doesn't know anything about my own particular issues – she knows I can't sleep sometimes, but aside from that I have shared nothing with her. "Are you ready to hit the town? I have just been checking that invitation, and apparently I need a dress. So, I was thinking, we could start at the mall, and then go down towards that place you mentioned? Then we can stop for lunch at the sandwich-bar when we're done shopping, too."

"Sure," I agreed. It sounded pretty good. "And then we can go back to your place?" I asked. She lived even closer to the mall than I did – we both had pretty centrally-placed accommodation, but I had chosen to live just a little further out – I couldn't handle the noise and the bright lights that close to our workplace.

"That's what I thought!" Neela agreed with a grin. "I even cleaned it."

"Neela," I teased, shoving her in the arm. "Your home is one of the cleanest I've ever seen. You make my place look positively untidy."

"No way," she said. "Just no way."

We were both laughing as we went downstairs and out through the front door. It was hot outside, which was nice – a warm, sweltering New York summer's day. I felt the heat make me start to sweat almost instantly and I was glad for my breezy dress. I glanced at Neela. She never showed any sign of being influenced by the weather – in all my years of knowing her I had never seen her look less than relaxed.

"So," she said as we walked down the busy street, weaving our way around people, trash-bins and chalkboards outside retro-looking restaurants. "We'll start upstairs at the mall and work our way down, okay?"

"Okay," I said with a shrug. I hoped it wouldn't be too desperately crowded – being in crowds can trigger me. I followed her in through the big door and up the escalator, glad that the real crowds hadn't seemed to have descended yet. Or, if they had, they were all still downstairs and not up on the top floor. Maybe her idea made sense, after all.

We spotted a clothing-shop and went in. I have to admit that I really do like shopping. Especially if I have a friend with me. I hadn't got nearly enough opportunities to do so lately, and I looked around, heart racing.

"So, what kind of a dress are you looking for?" I asked her.

She shrugged. "Something cool, a bit revealing. I plan to have a really good tan by then."

"Neela!" I chuckled. "When is the party?"

"Week after next." She grinned. "If needed, I shall go to a tanning bed. The ends justify the means, after all."

I had to laugh. That was typical of her! I shook my head, grinning at her. "You know those things are probably not good for you."

"Probably not," she said with a shrug. "I don't reckon that every once in a while will kill me, though."

"No, probably not," I agreed.

We went around the store, looking for where the dresses were. I stared at the bright colors, the delicate patterns. They had all their summer stock out already and my heart raced. There was a beautiful dress there, with the new stuff on one of the tall racks where they displayed the really nice – white with a pattern of flowers on the bodice, in soft purple, just the mauve side of lavender. I pointed, wordless.

Neela nodded. "You have to," she said.

I shook my head. "It's pretty expensive," I said, taking it off the rack. It was eighty dollars, which I guessed wasn't impossible for me, by any means, considering my recent pay-raise. All the same, I have always been really bad at spending money. Especially for myself.

"No, it isn't," Neela said firmly. "It's great quality. Just feel it." She ran her hand down the soft, silky skirt. I did the same. It was a lovely texture, and I could see how well-made and cut it was. It was actually worth the price. "You won't need to buy another dress this summer."

"Yeah…I guess so."

Neela saw me put it back, and gave me an angry look. "Come on," she said. "If I find something, you have to promise to buy that. I will not let you leave it."

I grinned. "Neela…" I said slowly. "Really, you can't expect me to spend so much on myself. I just can't."

"If I can do it, you have to," Neela said.

I sighed and she nodded. "Come on, you know I'm right. Let's go and look over there. I'm thinking of something pale, to show off my tan."

"Your soon-to-be-acquired tan," I agreed, laughing.

She nodded. We spent all morning in the mall. Finally, on the last floor we visited, Neela found a shop with a dress she liked. It was long, straight and with thin straps, made of a heavy white fabric that fell to her ankles. We tried it on in the dressing-room together and I had to applaud her good judgment.

"Wow," I said.

"I'm taking it," she said, grinning. She looked at the price-tag. "And it's way more expensive than the one you liked. So now you absolutely have to take it."

"Okay," I said. I watched her shrug off the dress and reach for her everyday clothes. The dress did look glamorous and stunning on her, with her black hair and those beautiful almost-black eyes. I wondered what the white-and-purple dress might look like.

"Come on," Neela said as we left the store, her dress in a paper bag, looped over one arm. "We're not leaving."

"Neela…" I said with a grin. I thought she had forgotten. I stopped walking. I actually felt ill when I thought about spending that much money on myself – and it wasn't even a work-dress. I couldn't really wear that to work. Why was I spending so much on it?

"I insist. Come on, Christina. I never see you do nice things for yourself. Now here I am, buying a ridiculously expensive dress just because I like it and, at the moment, I can afford to. I don't see any reason why you shouldn't do the same. What's that eighty dollars going to do for you if you don't spend it on something that'll make you happy?"

I sighed. I couldn't really explain to her how I felt. She would have dismissed it. I nodded.

"We can at least see how it looks," I agreed.

"Great!" she said. "Come on, then; let's go."

We went back and took the dress off the hook and Neela insisted on going with me into the changing-room to try it on. I looked at my reflection.

"Oh. Heck…I guess it does look nice, in a way…"

"It looks beautiful. And you're getting it. Or I'm going to get it and give it to you as a gift."

"Neela!" I looked at her, eyes wide. She wasn't joking, and I knew. It was just the sort of thing she would do. "I'll buy it."

"Great!" she said. She grinned. "Sorry. I didn't mean to push you. I just know what you're like. You would save all your money and never have any fun with it if I didn't try and push you into enjoying it every now and again."

"Yeah, I guess," I agreed.

"I know," she said. "Let's go and buy it."

I went to the checkout, and it took real effort to take the cash out and pay for it. I felt queasy as I stood there, but after I'd bought it, I actually felt great.

"I'm glad I got it," I told Neela, as we walked back to her place after having our sandwiches at the little sandwich-bar around the corner from our workplace.

"Yeah, so am I," said Neela. "Now, let's go and do those manicures. And you can help me decide how to accessorize this dress. I have had it up to here with coordinating color."

I laughed and we went back up to her flat.

I left after a few hours, with my head spinning from strong coffee – Neela always made us coffee, and I was dizzy for about an hour afterwards because of the strong brand she bought – my nails looking really beautiful and feeling relaxed.

I also had a beautiful dress, and I felt really good. I was looking forward to the rest of the week, after all.

Chapter 5: Christina

I walked into my office on Monday morning and stopped what I was doing as Mr. Caden walked in. I stared.

"Good morning," I said.

Under the circumstances, I thought it was quite impressive that I could find words. There was absolutely no reason for the CEO of our company to be standing in my office at 8 am on a Monday morning, looking at me with a slight lift of his lips that suggested a smile.

I waited for him to speak.

"Morning." He put his head on one side curiously, regarding me. "You're in early...I couldn't help noticing."

"Um, yeah," I said, shrugging. So, I was early – as far as I knew, that wasn't something I could be fired for, was it? I looked up at him, feeling uncomfortable. "You wanted to say something, Mr. Caden?"

He looked back at me, from where he had stared out of the window. It almost seemed like he was nervous, and I wondered what the heck he'd come in here for. He cleared his throat.

"Well, I was early too, and since you were in, I wanted to ask you how the software is working."

"The software?" I was bewildered. Which software? Was I supposed to be doing something with new software? I felt suddenly concerned – I must have forgotten to do something. All the same, he didn't seem annoyed with me.

I saw that he was looking at me expectantly, and instantly recalled the meeting, where he'd said he wanted us all to try the new software. I took a deep breath, calming down. "Um, I downloaded it. I haven't had much chance to play with it yet..." I trailed off vaguely. Why was he asking me? As it happened, I really had taken the chance to download it as soon as he sent the link. But it seemed weird that he was so interested in my opinion about it.

He grinned. "No worries," he said. "I mean, it isn't like you had any more board meetings that needed preparing and you needed to use it. I just wondered how you experienced it."

"Oh. Not bad," I said. I had looked at it for a bit, and the little I had done I had found really straightforward. "It's okay, actually. I found it pretty intuitive."

"Yeah," he said, nodding. "I also thought that. It does things the way you expect to."

"Yeah," I said.

He looked at me. I looked at him. I was sure he could see pretty clearly on my face that there was no way I understood what he was on about or why he was here. I was frankly confused. I was sure it showed on my face.

He lifted one shoulder, giving a shrug. "Okay, that's great." He nodded. "Well, I guess I should go and leave you to whatever busy things you were doing." He smiled a little nervously.

"Yeah, I guess."

We looked at each other and I was surprised to feel a tingle of something down my spine. I wasn't sure what it was, exactly, but it was a strange feeling. My heart raced and a strange shiver went down my spine. I pushed it away, feeling annoyed at myself.

"See you tomorrow," he said.

I frowned.

"Why tomorrow?" I asked. Then I remembered – we had an important meeting tomorrow – the joined meeting with the marketing guys. "Yeah, the meeting," I said. "See you tomorrow."

He smiled and walked out.

I gaped after him for a moment, completely confused.

"What was that about?"

I hurriedly got busy with something – I had some data to check that one of my colleagues had sent me. I was having a hard time focusing, though – my mind kept on going back to the strange incident with my boss.

Why had he come here, and acted so weirdly? He had always been rude and patronizing, and then, suddenly, just before a big meeting, he comes in and talks randomly about software? I had no idea what he was up to. It also annoyed me that I seemed to respond to him – or at least, that I actually enjoyed talking to him.

"I just feel unsettled," I told myself. That was what it was. It wasn't because I actually liked him. That definitely wasn't it – it couldn't be.

He was an annoying jerk. He always managed to say something disconcerting, and I didn't like the way I felt when he was around. I absolutely didn't.

"Hey," someone said from the door. I looked up to find my immediate junior in the doorway. His sandy hair indicated that he had showered and run straight to work – he hadn't brushed it and it was in quite a style. He looked worried.

"Hey, Millwall," I greeted him. For some reason, we all called him that. It was his surname. I hadn't actually asked anyone what his first name was, which was kind of bad of me. He looked worried.

"Christina," he said.

"Hey! Come in," I said, beckoning him over.

"May I sit down?"

"Sure," I agreed. I showed him the chair across the desk, a plastic one that isn't quite as nice as my own office chair. I felt a bit bad about that, but it wasn't like anyone had to sit there, and it wasn't my fault that we can't buy better furniture for the office, for some reason. He looked at me. "What's it?" I asked.

He coughed. "Um, Christina," he said haltingly. "I've been looking through the presentation, and there's something bothering me. I was wondering if you could explain it to me?"

"Sure," I said. I was pleased he'd asked – I had definitely been in situations as an office junior where I would have been too scared to admit I wasn't sure. I opened the presentation and tried to turn the screen, so we could both see. "What slide?"

"Um, slide nine," he said. "I was really struggling with the part where they show last year's expenditure. The way I worked it out, the totals should be different, and I can't see how they did it."

"Oh." I frowned. "Well, I got these slides from Benni – it was his job to work this bit out. He sent me the sheets. Let's look at them together, shall we?"

"Thanks, Christina," he said.

We looked at the figures together and I thought he was starting to understand. I could see how Benni had done the calculations and it made sense to me. I tried to explain it to him.

"So, you calculate the tax from the gross income. And then you take away the other expenses, including tax. I think I see where I went wrong..." Millwall nodded. "I think my sheet had the tax programmed in automatically, so I ended up with less income than I thought we made."

"Yeah," I nodded. "Sounds right. Would you like to show me the sheet? Or are you cool with it now?"

"Yeah, thanks." He smiled. "And thanks for taking time to talk that over with me. You're a great boss."

"Thanks," I said. I felt my heart warm. I had never thought of myself as a good boss. I had always thought of myself as not being able to handle being in charge. I had seen myself in the worst possible light, I was starting to think. "Glad you understand it now."

"I do now. I'm going to go and check through my calculations again. And I will send you the projections for tomorrow's meeting again if anything comes out a different value this time round!"

I chuckled. "I'm sure it will be fine," I said. "Let's talk about it this afternoon, when we go through the presentation, okay?"

"Great. Thank you!"

I felt good, leaning back in the chair after he'd left. Having been able to help with the calculations made me feel good. I liked being able to support the people who were now in a position where I had been five years ago. I always believed in being kind.

I felt my thoughts wander back to the paid internship I'd held. I had fought hard to make way for myself there – I'd been pretty intimidated by all the people in the company, and I felt like they somehow sensed that I wasn't from the same background as them and didn't get their references and jokes. I'd worked so hard just to try to blend in and not do anything that would single me out. I didn't want any of my employees to go through that.

I glanced back from the window to the door, just in time to see the departmental secretary hurrying up the hallway with a form. I remembered that I had to get something back to Burgess early. I signed it hastily.

"Great. Should I take it down to the boss now?"

"No. Thanks, but I need to check some stuff and then I'll go and take it back to the boss myself."

"Great! Thanks." She hurried out of my office, back to her desk, and I hastily read through the document, checking for any errors. I got it to Burgess just before five and then rushed back to my desk.

I was just going down the stairs, hurrying so that I might shave a few minutes off the time spent in traffic, when I came to a halt. Mr. Caden held up two hands.

"Heck! Sorry...I didn't know how fast you were going. Sorry...that was my fault."

"No, not at all," I said. We had almost collided, and I'd managed to stop short of knocking him over.

"It was my fault, really. You must be in a hurry...I'll let you off."

"Thanks," I said. I looked at him, trying to decide whether he was being an ass or whether he was being nice. With him I often found it pretty hard to tell. I could see an odd expression in his eyes and I didn't stick around to try and figure out what it was. I hate being stuck in traffic. I turned around and ran down the stairs.

"Have a good evening," I heard somebody say as I passed. I didn't stop to see who it was.

"Good evening!" I shouted over my shoulder. I ran to where I'd left my car and jumped in, turning the key with unnecessary strength. I knew there was something wrong with the engine and I was sure I was going to have to take it in to get it fixed, sometime soon. Right now, though, all that mattered was that it got me home.

I drove back, pleased to have avoided the worst of the traffic somehow.

When I got back to my apartment, I was surprised by how much Mr. Caden was on my mind. I wished I understood what was getting into him. He had spoken to me really nicely this morning, and even when I almost ran into him, he wasn't as rude as I would have expected, in fact he wasn't rude at all. I was still baffled by it, and turning the question over in my mind, when I fell asleep.

Chapter 6: Brett

I couldn't stop thinking about Christina. I was annoyed with myself – after all, I had a lot to do and I really had to be preparing for the big meeting tomorrow evening. I didn't need distractions right now.

And almost walking into Christina had been distracting.

I recalled her lovely figure – trim waist, generous curves, pale skin. I hadn't realized how much I longed to kiss that sweetly-perfumed skin, how I wanted to bury my face in her hair and breathe that elusive, fresh fragrance of her.

"Come on, Brett," I told myself sharply. This was no time for flights of imagination. I had a lot of work to do.

I was sitting in my sitting-room, just the other side of the open-plan kitchen. I am very fond of my apartment – it was a real surprise to find something so absolutely high-quality at a reasonable price. Well, okay, reasonable in terms of someone who is owner of a company that grossed three billion last year. But all the same, it was a bargain. Yes, I might have a multibillion-dollar company, but I didn't always have one, and I sometimes struggle with spending money a bit. I guess it was how I was brought up. My family had been comfortable, but not wealthy, and I sometimes struggled to accept my own wealth and the luxury of my surroundings.

I wasn't thinking of the beautiful granite floor or the stunning coffee-table, though. I was thinking of the beautiful face of my senior executive. She looked so surprised! This morning, when I had actually spoken to her in her office, she had clearly thought I was nuts.

I guess I was acting a bit weirdly, but I knew I couldn't help myself. If I had an opportunity to speak with her, I intended to take it. I leaned back on the couch, feeling restless.

"I guess I should tidy something."

I have a bad habit of leaving dishes in the sink. It is all very well until you can't put stuff in the sink anymore and you happen to have guests. That had happened to me once, and it was very embarrassing. I went through to put the dishes away.

As I dried the plates, I found myself thinking about the meeting tomorrow. My own part was to convince the board, while Christina would be presenting the current and future state of the company, and the marketing guys would do their presentation about how we were going to market it. I thought about Christina doing the presentation. Or rather, I thought about Christina.

"Damn it," I muttered to myself, though I was grinning as I walked through to the black granite tiles. I was amused by how she was never far from my mind.

I pushed away images of Christina in a tight shirt and black skirt. It was what she had been wearing the other day. I absolutely wasn't going to stare at her gorgeous body, I was there to listen to the talks.

I finished tidying the kitchen, and remembered to call my brother. I had been meaning to call him for ages, but until now I hadn't had any time. I sat down and phoned.

"Hey! Teagan," I greeted him. "How's it?"

"Okay," he replied, stifling a yawn. "Not bad. How are you?"

"Good, good. Busy but not as busy as I should be; that sort of day."

"Sounds good," Teagan said.

"Maybe," I replied with a shrug. I have always found it a bit tricky talking to Teagan. He was a champion baseball player, and since an injury to his knee he has since gone into being a spokesperson and advisor for sports facilities planning. He earns well, but I have always worried that maybe he has a grudge against me – though he has never said anything of the sort before. I had made a lot of money, while his glittering career had suffered a setback. And it was a difficult thing to address because I was always intimidated by him as a kid – he was such a big figure in sports. "It was quite a tiring day," I added, feeling myself yawn.

"Well, I can agree with you if you've had enough of meetings," he said with a grin. "I have had a week full of them. We're talking about budgets. You know...it really annoys me how these politicians always talk about money. You'd think their job was to save the country money, not to serve us."

"Yeah," I nodded. "It must be pretty frustrating." I was interested in his work, but we worked in such different sectors that it was not always easy to talk about stuff. I wished I could really connect with him and talk about everyday things, like how I felt about Christina. I was a bit shy of discussing that sort of stuff with him – maybe because girls had always hung around him when we were young, but none of them really seemed to notice his little brother.

"Well, I guess it's what I do," he said with a sigh, his comment bringing me back to the moment. "How were your meetings and stuff? Tiring, I guess."

"Yeah," I said. "Probably less stressful than yours. Different sort of meetings, really. Though not that different. Still about money, and how to get it out of people." I chuckled, self-deprecatingly.

"No, probably not that different," he agreed with a laugh. "You mentioned you had a big one coming up."

"Yeah," I said. "I should probably look into that a bit more this evening. I guess I am just tired." I felt another yawn coming on.

"Have you had dinner?" he asked. I chuckled.

"I've started cooking something. I know I sometimes forget." I often came back late from the office after meetings and didn't have dinner. Not intentionally, just because I was too tired.

"Brett, I know you know how bad that is," he said, concernedly. "You need to have enough energy, you know. You burn more than you think just using your brain."

"Yeah, I know," I agreed. "I know I need to eat. I really do just forget."

"Yeah. Well, if I invite you for dinner, you don't have any excuse. Will you come down next week?"

"Um, yeah," I agreed. It was a surprise that he would invite me for dinner – I always had the impression he was too busy to have dinner with me. Or that he didn't really like my company.

"Great," my brother said. "I'll see you then."

"See you, bro."

We hung up. It felt good, having spoken to my brother. He was oddly reassuring in my life. After all, he was a big star way before I had my company. My company shot up rather swiftly – being a billionaire and CEO by the time you are thirty-one is weird, and anyone would need somebody as a sort of advisory role. Something like a father figure, without the scary authority connotations. That was Teagan, for me. Our own father had separated from our mother when we were both young, and Teagan had more or less taken over his role in my life by the time I left home.

It would be nice, I thought, to have dinner with him.

I finished tidying the kitchen and went through to my room.

I looked around, a small smile lifting my lip as I took in the soft carpet, the white walls and designer furniture, the bed with its pure cotton covers. I was sure that lots of people thought that I got up to all sorts of bad-boy stuff in this bedroom, but really, all I did in bed was check budget reports and sleep. I had never actually been much of a one for wild parties, though the press tended to speculate, at a low level, about me, and I let them.

It didn't hurt to let people think I was getting up to all sorts, with all sorts of people.

I suppose people expect bad behavior from the rich and sort-of famous, but I was really quite boring – I had a few long-term girlfriends, but mostly they had been people my family more-or-less directed me at: relatives of my school friends and college friends, people my parents had thought were the "proper" girlfriends for me. I hadn't fallen in love before. I wondered idly if I ever would.

I reached for my book, then I put it aside and went to shower. I let the warm water sluice over my body and I found myself thinking about Christina. I imagined her here with me, her lovely butt pressed against my naked belly, her curvy thighs stroking up against me as I reached around and ran my hands down her wet skin, reaching lower and lower.

I imagined my cock hard and thick as I pushed against her back, my hands moving around to her belly and moving lower, rubbing between her thighs as she gasped in surprise.

"Oh, come off it," I told myself aloud as I stepped out of the shower. I was hopelessly aroused.

There was no way I should be thinking like that.

I was going to be sitting across a table from her tomorrow! If I was visualizing her naked, it wasn't going to do any good at all. I had to be focused. I tried to get the image out of my mind but my body was pretty fixated.

I got into bed and lay back on the soft, warm pillows and tried to think. I had an important meeting tomorrow and I needed to sleep. I absolutely did not need my mind filled with crazy images of one of the staff who would probably slap me half-silly if I asked. She was absolutely not what I needed to be focused on.

I reached for my book and tried to read.

Chapter 7: Brett

I drove home, unable to stop thinking about Christina. I had so enjoyed talking to her. In that situation, after the meeting, she acted different. I was used to her being so distant, so cold, and I would never have expected her to be actually friendly to me. But she had been so nice!

And yes, I had to admit to myself that I had been staring at her the whole afternoon; watching her lovely face as she spoke, and letting my eyes wander down her gorgeous chest and back up. Yes, she had a lovely body, with those gorgeous curves, but it wouldn't have got to me without her personality. It was her surprising warmth and her quick temper that made her so sexy.

"Hell...this is really silly." I told myself as I looked into the mirror, giving myself a stern talking-to. I really wasn't supposed to fall for an employee. It was something that I had never really safeguarded against, because it was something I had never thought would happen to me.

I went and made myself some tea. I sat down on the couch to drink it. I wished I could tell Teagan about how I felt about my employee, but I didn't think it was something he'd understand. He'd either tell me to go for it, or tell me to forget about it.

And I didn't really want to do either.

I drained my tea and tried to put Christina out of my mind.

"She would never even look at me."

I remembered how she had suddenly tensed and turned away, practically running from me to get away. I still didn't know what I'd said. I was probably making it a bit too clear how attracted I was, and that scared her.

I leaned back and looked up at the ceiling. I was tired, but not tired enough to go to bed. I walked over to the kitchen, reminding myself that I hadn't eaten yet. I opened the freezer to find some pre-baked quiche. I bought them from a particular little boutique food store around the corner. I know what I like, and what I eat is something I am willing to spend quite a lot of money on.

I put that in the oven to heat and, after I had eaten, I went to go and take a shower. I usually take a shower twice a day, if I can. I like to clear away the stress of the day before I get some sleep. In the shower, I found my mind straying to Christina again. I imagined her lovely hand where my hand was, stroking between my thighs. Her fingers were beautiful – long and elegant, with short nails. I imagined her touching me, and I felt my eyes squeeze shut with the ache of desire I felt for her.

I turned up the shower, giving myself a thorough soaking. I was really being silly now. How was I supposed to look her in the eye if I was standing here feeling myself to thoughts of her?

I dried myself off and slipped into bed. I really had to do something about this. I needed to distract myself somehow. I could guess what Teagan would say – he would tell me I was just desperate because I hadn't been with a woman in ages. Maybe he was right, but I didn't think so. I didn't just want somebody for the sake of wanting somebody. I felt something for Christina – an interest that I couldn't simply turn off. I liked her.

If she had liked me, I would even ask her out, I thought – yes, I knew it was frowned on to date people from your company, but it certainly wasn't impossible and I would be fine with it: If she was.

I rolled over and drew the covers up around my shoulders. I really should stop thinking about her – after all, I'd reached out and tried to be friendly, but she had definitely made her opinion clear. I couldn't challenge that.

I drove to work after a good breakfast – I always believe in starting the day full of energy – and found myself wondering about the meeting that afternoon. I was a little late when I arrived – the traffic had been worse than I thought – and I hurried up the hallway to my office. I stopped, cursing, as I walked into a crate. My toe ached. I bent down and then, when I straightened up, after checking my toe was still attached, I found myself looking straight at Christina.

"Sorry," I hissed. My toe was throbbing and I wished I could clear my head. It was hard to think when everything was so very painful. "I was just hurrying along, and I bumped into this...thing." I gestured at the wooden crate – I didn't want to let out the stream of curses that were neatly held back behind my teeth.

"It's the new equipment. Sorry," Christina said. She gestured at a delivery man who was standing next to us, his eyes stretched to big rounds as he watched us talking to each other. "It's okay. Can you move it into that room, please?"

"Yes, ma'am. Immediately."

I turned to Christina. I wasn't sure what she thought. If she had any sense, she'd probably burst out laughing – after all, I must have looked funny, no matter how sore it was. Instead, she looked up at me, eyes wide.

"Can I get you something? You must be in pain."

"Yeah, I am a bit." I tried to grin. "It's stupid, isn't it? Toes always hurt so damn much. Sorry," I added, realizing that I'd sworn.

She shrugged. "I'd say worse than that if it was my toe," she said.

We shared a grin. I recalled the previous day, when we'd talked so happily, until she turned away like that and seemed to be almost afraid of me. I wished I knew what had happened. Now, I let her lead me into the printing-room. I sat down. It was a relief to be off my feet. My toe was still throbbing and I was tempted to see what had happened to it.

"You should see what happened," Christina said, coming and standing opposite me. She looked down at my foot, a small frown lowering her brows.

"Maybe," I said. I hesitated to undo my shoe with her there. I knew it was silly, but I was self-conscious. What if I had weird feet? I didn't want her to judge me. I was wearing socks, though, and I guessed I could at least take off my shoe.

I untied my shoelaces and the relief was instant. I took off my shoe. She sat down opposite me. When I looked up, she was looking at my face.

"Does that feel better?" she asked.

I nodded. Suddenly, I was aware of the fact that I was sitting opposite a beautiful woman, in the printing-room, my shoe off and my sock-clad foot in my hand. The strangeness of the situation was overwhelming, but oddly, with her, it didn't feel embarrassing. I grinned at her, feeling shy.

"I guess it was pretty dumb to walk into that thing, hey?"

"Not at all!" Christina said. "You have every reason not to expect a gigantic box in the middle of your hallway."

I laughed. "Yeah, I guess so." I frowned. "Your hallway, actually – it goes past your office."

"It's your company, Mr. Caden."

I shrugged. "It is, yeah," I said. Weirdly, I didn't feel that comfortable with that, right now. I would rather have been the guy delivering stuff – at least then I could have honestly made a pass at Christina without anybody thinking I was using my influence to coerce her. And without me having to worry that I could do so, if I wanted to.

She was watching me. Her brown eyes examined mine and I didn't think that she was angry with me anymore – I had wondered, after we had talked last night and she had hurried away so quickly, if she was mad with me. But now, all I could see in her eyes was sympathetic gentleness.

It was nice to see – I don't see people give me that look very often, in fact I couldn't think that anyone else had ever given me that look ever.

I let out a sigh.

"I guess I should get back to work," Christina said. "Are you sure I can't get you a painkiller or something?"

"It's okay," I said, hastily putting on my shoe. Luckily, I was wearing neutral gray socks. Nothing with any embarrassing pictures or slogans on them. "I don't need anything. It is going off."

"Good," she nodded.

We looked at each other. She was looking at me with those beautiful dark eyes and I realized, again, that she was within easy reach of me and that I could so easily reach out and touch her. She smiled, her pale lips lifting in the sweetest grin. I felt my heart ache. Her hand rested on the chair beside her and, as I stood, I reached out and touched it.

"Thank you," I said. "You helped me."

"I didn't, really," Christina said honestly. "All I did was tell you to sit down and take your shoe off."

I smiled. "You didn't laugh, which really helped me."

"I couldn't have laughed when you were in pain," she said.

"No." I nodded. "That's very nice of you."

She shrugged awkwardly. I could see that her old discomfort was back and I could understand that – I felt on edge too. People were starting to come up the hallway, and someone else came in to get printing from the desk. I straightened up. My shoe was on; I just needed to tie it.

"Thanks for helping me," I said softly as I went to the door. "I'll see you later today."

"See you later," she whispered.

I went up the hallway and I had to admit that my heart was thumping. I felt happy, and a little dazed. I still couldn't quite believe I had been sitting there so naturally, talking to Christina. I walked up to my office, passing my secretary, who called out to me.

"Mr. Camden? You have a meeting today at ten."

"I know. Thanks for reminding me. I'll be ready in a moment."

I strode into my office and sat down. My toe still hurt, but I could barely recall the actual wound. I was lost in thoughts of Christina – her sweet face, her beautiful body encased in that gray blouse and slacks. I ached to draw her against me, to cover her soft mouth with kisses. I imagined how it would feel to kiss her, my tongue pushed between those soft lips.

"Mr. Caden? Telephone – it's Mr. Rawlinson, from the board."

"Put him through…I'll talk to him now."

I was still having trouble thinking about Mr. Rawlinson and the budget. I was thinking about Christina and her soft mouth, and how she would melt in my arms as I pressed her back onto the sheets…

"So, Brett. That new investment. You'll be needing four hundred thousand from each of us?"

"Um, yeah," I said. He had certainly brought me back to the present, in no uncertain way. I blinked, trying to think properly. "Yes, that's right."

"And you calculate return on investments is fifteen-fold in five years. Yeah?"

"Yes, that's it." I was lucky that I was good at remembering numbers. I had memorized all the pertinent values from the meeting yesterday; and in any case, I knew the numbers for this project very well.

"Sounds good. I just wanted to check it, because my gut tells me something different."

"What?" I frowned. "Mr. Rawlinson, could you be a bit clearer on that? What does your gut tell you?"

"It tells me there's something off in the expenditure. It's not possible that it's going to become profitable that quick. Not with what you were telling us yesterday. No…something's off. I am assuming right now that someone screwed up. Am I right?"

"Um, possibly," I said slowly. What else could I say? I tried to think. "I'm going to call a meeting with the finance guys later this afternoon anyway. I'll discuss it then and can I call to inform you this evening?"

"I'd prefer it if you check it out now. That's a lot of money, and if I'm right, your ROI is out by quite a lot. Can you go and talk to your finance guy?"

"Sure," I said. I stood up, ready to do and do it. "I'll see him right away."

"Good. And tell me afterwards. I like you, Brett, and I don't like to think that you're trying to kid anybody."

I felt sick. What had happened? I had checked those figures myself! I had checked them so many times. I didn't understand what he meant – and I especially didn't like the thought that board-members thought my aim was to extract cash from them on false premises.

I stood and went out to find my head of finance.

I strode through to his office, my sore foot utterly forgotten. I tapped at the door. He was talking to an employee, but he saw something in my posture and he turned to the guy, speaking softly.

"I think I need to chat with our CEO quickly. If you could come back in half an hour?"

"Sure," the young man said. He looked at me, looked nervous and went out through the door. I went in and shut the door behind me.

"What the hell happened to the spreadsheets you sent me?" I asked him.

"Which spreadsheets?" His full-jawed face seemed calm. He was a big man, my head of finance – not in a soft way, but in a way that suggested he could give a serious punch. I liked him. I trusted him. But I was annoyed that a mistake had slipped through.

"The ones that calculate return on investments," I managed to say somehow. I was furious. "Can you talk me through them? Show me how they work?"

"Sure," he said. He gestured me to a seat behind his desk. I came over and sat down. He joined me at the computer; clicked on the spreadsheets, which were on the desktop, calling them up.

"This is the same file you sent me," I asked. I wanted to be sure. He nodded.

"Yes, the same. Now, if you look here, this is the column where I work out the expenditure. In the first year, it's given using these values, here..." He scrolled down to show me a separate table, where the evaluations for the different publications were written. I frowned as I read through them. None of it made sense. I would need hours to sit and work through all of that, and I didn't have hours right now. I looked at him.

"This needs checking," I said flatly. "Somebody has messed up here. Or, if they haven't, I need a report as to how they haven't. And I need it by the end of the week."

"It's only two days from now," he said.

"Yes, I know," I confirmed. "But I need that work done. The board is angry. Someone thinks we screwed up."

"Who?" Burgess asked me. I ran a hand down my face.

"Why does it matter who it was?" I asked.

"If it was Rawlinson, you know he's a pain in the..."

"It was Rawlinson, yeah, but it doesn't matter who it was," I said carefully. "And this is not a moment to be insulting members of the board, no matter how much we might want to. I want to as well, trust me. But there are other people listening." I gestured at the door.

He sighed. "Yeah, I suppose. You can never be sure who's listening around here. But come on, Brett. You don't really think I did this on purpose, do you?"

"Of course not," I said quickly. I didn't think that. I had worked with Burgess for the last five years – since a little bit before that, actually, right back when I was establishing our company. He was trustworthy, of that I didn't have any doubt. I sometimes found him quick-tempered and a bit too careless for my liking, but I had no cause to think he would actually lie to the board.

"Well, I'll try and get you that report. We're going to need the rest of the week, though. That much I can tell you. And if Rawlinson tries to get funny, you tell him that I'll give him a report where he's never had a report before."

I had to smile. "I won't pass that on, no. But I will inform him he will need patience."

"You do that," Burgess said. He raised a brow and I went to the door.

"Thank you, Burgess. I'll go and talk to him immediately."

He nodded and I went off up the hallway, going to my office. I sat for a moment and tried to compose myself – I was still a little shocked, if I was honest, by the accusation he had made. Rawlinson, that was. I had not planned what to do if someone accused me of cheating, because, to be honest, nobody had ever accused me of not being truthful.

"Mr. Rawlinson," I greeted as he answered the phone. "This is Brett Caden. I just spoke with my finance officer, and he informs me that everything looks accurate to him. He is preparing a report, which I will issue to you and to the rest of the board – whoever is interested – on Friday."

"Good. Good, Brett," he said. "I am glad you'll be doing that. I am still wondering how he worked that out – there's no way those particular magazine titles could be as profitable as that."

"Okay," I said. I wasn't going to comment or defend. "I think we should wait for the end of the week when the report arrives."

"Yeah. We'll wait for them. I'll be very interested to read that."

"Good," I said.

I put the phone down. I was shaking with some emotion I didn't understand. It was anger, I thought. And shock. I had never been accused of trying to deceive my board-members before. I couldn't understand why Rawlinson had got this into his head. I went through to talk to my secretary.

"Caley, please don't send me anybody or any calls right now. I will go to the meeting at two, but before then I need to be undisturbed. Is that good?"

"Yes, Mr. Caden. I'll tell them you're busy."

"Thanks."

I went into my office and locked the door. I really didn't want to be disturbed right now. I needed time to clear my head and think. Oddly, I wished I could talk to Christina about it. She was in finance, so she wouldn't be too bad to talk to anyway. And when I'd hurt my toe so badly, she had been so understanding.

I wished I could tell her about this situation with the board. I felt sure she would understand, but I couldn't tell her because she was a senior executive and, if I could, I wanted to let as few people know about this as possible. Just myself and Burgess, and whoever would help him with the report. Those were the only people whom it was necessary to tell.

I leaned back in my chair and checked my emails, trying to focus on something other than that report and how important it was to convince the board of my intentions.

Chapter 8: Christina

I was sitting in my office, quietly calming down after the finance meeting, when my boss came to call. I had noticed he seemed a little tense – during the meeting, he had been sitting rigidly, answering questions as if he was on trial for something really awful. I had wondered if there was something bothering him.

"Christina...I need to talk to you."

"Okay," I said, raising one shoulder in a shrug. "Sounds good to me. What's up?"

"Christina...we need to talk privately. Can you come?"

"Sure," I said. He walked into his office and when I was inside, he shut the door. Already, I was feeling pretty alarmed. I really didn't need someone shutting me into their office. It was just the sort of thing to put me in a really bad space. I looked at him.

"Christina, I need a report done. And it has to be done the day after tomorrow."

"What?" I stared. "What report is it?" I asked. It couldn't be anything demanding – if it was a summary of something we'd already done, that sounded reasonable. I could do that. It would be extra work, but if it was something simple, it certainly wouldn't bother me.

"I need a report written from the beginning – to describe all our calculations for the financial projections for the new venture. Everything has to be done transparently, so that the board can see why our return on investments is so big."

"What?" I swayed on my feet. That wasn't just some extra work – that was a massive task. And it needed to be done in a few days? That wasn't sounding like something I could do, unless I could have my juniors working alongside for the two days – we could get it done together in that time, I guessed.

"I am sorry, Christina. But it needs to be strictly confidential, which is why I came to you. I knew that you would be able to do it alone, without needing to tell anybody what we're doing."

"What?" Now I was furious. This was just wrong! How could he expect me to do such a huge task alone? I hadn't even done all of the projections – some of them were his! How I was supposed to explain stuff when I hadn't done stuff was a mystery to me. I looked at him.

"I know you can do it," he said firmly. "I know you will do it, because I can recommend someone to take over when I finally retire, and I know that I would recommend you if you do this for me."

"You are literally threatening me," I said. My heart pounded. I felt sick. How could he do this to me? He hadn't actually threatened me, but it felt like it.

He shrugged. "I just said I'd recommend you if you did it," he said. "I don't see a threat there. Now, I expect to see that report the day after tomorrow."

"You can expect it if you want," I said, finally losing my temper. "You can't get it."

"Well, if you can't do it by then, I will wonder whose projections were wrong."

Now I really was angry. He meant that he would blame me for everything if I didn't do this. And then I would be in danger. I had no way to avoid what he was requiring me to do.

"Fine," I said. "I'll do it. But I won't trust anything from you again."

He nodded. He seemed perfectly calm. I was sure that he had every reason not to worry – after all, I was no threat to him, but he was a huge threat to me and he knew it.

I went into my office, sat down and tried to be calm.

"Okay," I told myself firmly. "It can't be that hard. Why would it be that hard? I can copy and paste bits out of the report we've already done and just expand on them – it can't possibly be that difficult; not really."

I opened the files he had sent me – the ones where he had done the calculations. I tried to understand what he had done and how he had done it. I was struggling.

"What the heck is that about, and why would he do it that way, anyway?" I asked myself, quite loudly.

I worked through my normal leaving-time. I was still working when my boss put his head in to say that he was leaving, and to ask me how it was going.

"Christina, you can finish it tomorrow. Really – go home and get some rest."

"No," I said. I was determined to finish. I was going to do it as soon as possible and get it out of the way so I didn't have to worry about it for the rest of the week.

"Okay," he said. He left. I felt better after he had gone. I shut the door and put the lights on and considered making some coffee. If I was going to be here all night, I might as well stay sensible.

I made some progress, and the report was starting to grow. It was getting dark outside. I stood up to close the curtain. I was starting to feel a little nervous. I had never actually worked in this building late on my own. It wasn't a nice feeling and I focused harder on my work, trying to ignore the fact that I needed something to drink and my water-glass had been empty for a while.

I absolutely didn't want to go out into that hallway.

Suddenly, I was thirteen and terrified again. My dad had come back from the gambling hall and he was swearing and cursing, stumbling up the hallway, trying to switch on the lights and getting frustrated and angry. He was shouting, kicking at the door. I could hear him shouting and I knew that if I went out into the hallway, something would happen. I needed to stay in my room. I needed to be quiet.

If I did everything right he wouldn't shout at me. I needed to stay where I was and be still so that nobody would hurt me. If I did everything right, I would be safe.

I started crying.

I didn't know why – I guess maybe the situation with my boss, and the assignment...it was all so similar, in its way, to how I felt as a child, hiding in my room so nobody would hurt me.

I knelt on the floor, sobs racking my body. I didn't want to go out into that hallway. I was tired. I was scared. I had so much to do and if I didn't get it right, someone would hurt me.

I was kneeling on the floor, sobbing, the tears running down my cheeks that had been inside me since I was small, that had been held frozen because it was dangerous to make a noise.

I knew the situation wasn't the same, but I was tired and it was late and it was so similar that my brain was acting as it had when I was little. I straightened up, sniffing. I thought I had heard a noise.

The instant tension in my body; the huge fear that washed through me because I thought there might really be someone out there made me sob more. I was so scared, so unable to hold my tears back. I rolled up with my knees to my chest, my arms wrapped around them, wishing I could just feel safe.

Suddenly, the door opened.

I shot upright, ready to defend myself, my heart pounding sheer terror through my body. I stared as someone looked at me, eyes wide with concern.

"Christina?" Mr. Caden said. "What happened?"

"I was...crying. Sorry," I said. I sniffed. My face was wet and I ran my hand across it, feeling the color drain from me. It was so embarrassing! I stared at him. He was looking at me, brown eyes wide. I had expected to see ridicule there, but instead I saw tenderness and sadness.

"Christina," he said gently. "Please, come out of here. Come into my office. What happened?"

I sniffed. The lights were on in the hallway. It was inviting and warm. I followed him out of my office – where the terror had been so real – and up the bright, carpeted hallway that was empty, now, of people. We went across and up to where the big white desk where his secretary sat separated his door from the rest of us.

He stood back for me, opening the door so I could go in before him.

"Christina," he said gently, as he followed me in. He shut the door behind me. I looked around and sat down on the leather chair across from his computer. He sat down on a stool, almost so close that our knees touched. I ignored that – I was too tired for the moment to think about it.

"I'm sorry," I said. It was the only word in my mind just then. I kept on repeating it. I felt so stupid. What would he think? That I was crazy. I was sure he had already decided that I was a poor senior executive and that he was already wondering how to shoulder me into another position. "Sorry. I was just tired. I shouldn't have been crying."

"Christina," he said gently. "Why would you say that? Of course, you should have been. The problem is with whatever made you cry, not with you."

I looked up. Weirdly, that was something that had never occurred to me. Where I came from, it was your reactions that were wrong, not whatever had made you unhappy. I found myself looking into his lovely brown eyes. He was full of tenderness and compassion.

"I shouldn't have been losing it like that at work," I said. I sniffed. I reached for something to wipe my nose. He passed me a piece of kitchen paper towel. Our fingers touched and I was surprised by the tingle that went through my arm and rushed all the way to my mind.

"It's almost eight at night, Christina," he said gently. "It's not work anymore. How long have you been here?"

"Since this morning?" I smiled. I tried to dry my face. I was sure he thought I was crazy, but he hadn't said anything about that fact.

He chuckled. "Hell, Christina! I do give you a tough job. What the heck have you been doing in there since nine a.m. this morning?"

I sniffed. "I don't think I'm supposed to talk about it. Confidential." I sniffed, blowing my nose.

He looked at me, his eyes wide. I could see gentleness there, and confusion. He coughed, clearing his throat. He had a beautiful mouth, I noticed – well-made lips, soft but well-formed. I felt my heart start to thump. I was tired.

"Christina, I am the company head. I don't think you need to keep it secret from me."

I blew my nose, trying to think of what to say. If I told him about the mess-up, maybe Burgess would be angry with me. But at the same time, he should know.

"I had to do a report. And fix some calculations," I said. I found myself looking into his eyes.

He smiled. "I think that whatever it was, it can't be that urgent," he said gently. "You are so tired. You shouldn't be working so late."

"I'm not tired," I snapped. I didn't want to be angry, but I felt like he didn't understand what had just happened. I knew that was ridiculous, but I was tired and my mind wasn't doing the best thinking at that precise moment. "I am overworked, frightened and exhausted. I am trying my best to do something that someone has told me to do, which is impossible." I drew a breath. "And I need to do it or nobody will ever think well of me again."

I couldn't stop crying. I knew he was there, and that it was inappropriate to cry like this in front of him, but I couldn't help it. Almost twenty years of pain were welling up inside me, unable to be held back anymore.

"It's okay," I heard someone say. Suddenly, I was being held in someone's strong arms, the scent of cologne and cotton suddenly overwhelming me. I wrapped my arms around him and held him and for the first time ever, I felt safe. "It's okay. It's okay."

I let those words sink into me and I held Brett Caden and he held me and let me cry. I slowly felt the tears start to lessen. I could sit up now. I leaned back, and felt his arms gently unfurl from around me. Slowly, as I stopped crying, I became aware of other things. How his knees pressed to mine. How his hands held mine. How he looked into my eyes, the tenderness mixed, now, with a strange interest.

I felt my heart start to thud. This time, the feelings that washed through me were not sadness. Or fear. I was looking into his eyes and feeling my body warm with heat that I had not felt in years. My heart was racing and I felt warmth flood throughout my body.

I thought that he was feeling something too. He was looking at me and the depths of his brown eyes were lit with an intensity of feeling that made my face flush. He took my hand and then, suddenly, he was leaning towards me and I was leaning towards him and our lips were meeting and we kissed.

I felt his soft, warm lips move onto mine, his tongue gently stroking across my own, seeking entrance. I felt my own lips part under his tongue, and it slid in and out again, carefully, teasingly tasting. His mouth tasted of warmth and mint and some slight musky taste that was uniquely him. I wrapped my arms around him and drew him closer and he held me and I could feel his hands on my back, even as my own were moving down his back, feeling the thick muscle that corded it.

He stood up and I stood too, our lips still together, our bodies pressing together with an urgency that raced through me. I drew him closer, feeling his hard, lean body against mine, the cool fabric of his shirt under my hands, his thick muscle beneath.

"Christina," he whispered.

I looked into his eyes and I could see longing there; the same longing that was washing through me. I felt my heart race. This feeling was like nothing I had ever dreamed I would experience; nothing like my mind could encompass.

We embraced again. I was aware of the deep longing coursing through me, making me tighten my grip on him as he kissed me, my body and his both moving together, pressing on each other with a clear intent. I could feel his hips on mine and I wanted to push against him as his hands stroked to my lower back, just where my blouse and trousers met.

He was holding me, his lips pressed to mine, his body and mine grasped so close to each other that I could feel his breath as I breathed my own.

He looked into my eyes and I nodded. I wanted this as much as he did.

We grinned at each other, breathless and a little bit surprised, I thought, by our collective daring. It started to feel a little unreal to me as we walked through the door and down the stairs. Then, at the bottom of the stairs, he embraced me again, his lean body hard on mine and I knew that I wanted him more than anything.

We went down to his car. It was in the cellar – a parking-area reserved for the CEO and the other chief executive officers. I followed him to his car, parked by the front gate. It was a black BMW and I slipped into the interior and then he was sitting beside me, his body pushing against me as he kissed me, our hands straying from stroking backs to pressing breasts and stroking down between my thighs.

I gasped as he touched me. My need for him was urgent. His hand was between my thighs and I pressed against him, wanting him so much that I could barely hold back. He was looking into my eyes, his own body suffering as mine was with the longing we experienced.

He straightened up, grinning at me. "I think I should drive," he said.

I nodded.

He moved so that he was sitting at the steering wheel and we drove through the darkened streets, the city quieting down as we moved from the busy downtown and towards the leafier part of town which he seemed to find more relaxing and familiar.

Chapter 9: Christina

I followed Brett into his apartment. It was dark, and he switched on the light, drawing me against him and kissing me hard. I could feel his arousal and I wanted him so much. It was so hard not to start undressing him in the hallway, but I sensed that he wanted to wait.

I looked around over his shoulder, seeing a super-stylish sitting-room with a leather couch and a beautiful stone floor, but then Brett was kissing my neck and I gasped, leaning against him. I could feel his cock through the fabric of his trousers – thick and firm and hard. I felt my own loins heat up with fresh longing.

His hands moved to my buttocks, and I shut my eyes as he squeezed them gently, drawing me against his hardness. I wanted him so much it was almost painful, yet he seemed to want to move more slowly.

He stepped back, and I thought he was almost shy as he gestured at the sitting-room.

"This is my apartment," he said.

I nodded. I looked around, taking in the elegant beige-and-stone interior. I looked up at him. It was a lovely apartment, but with him in it, a dingy hotel room would have been stunning. I wrapped my arms around him and his lips found mine and the arousal threatened to overwhelm me as he slowly moved his hands down my body, squeezing my waist, slowly stroking my back, moving down to my buttocks and then back to the soft skin at the back of my neck, touching it with a teasing finger.

"Brett," I murmured, as he found my lips again, his own firm on mine as he tasted me. I had my eyes shut, enjoying the sensation of his hard, eager mouth on mine.

His hands moved again to my buttocks, drawing me against him, letting me feel his hardness and how much he wanted me as I pushed eagerly against him.

He gently tugged me sideways, drawing me towards the bedroom. I followed him. He shut the door behind us and then his hands were on my body, gripping my waist, drawing me against him as he kissed me, stroking my hair.

I kissed him, hands smoothing his back, feeling his hard muscle. He moved slightly, making me tip over and then, giggling, I collapsed onto the bed, him landing beside me with his arm under me.

"Christina."

He looked into my eyes and gently rolled onto me, my body under his as he kissed me, his weight pressing me down into the softness of the bed. I could feel his fingers slipping into my shirt, touching my breasts through the fabric of my bra. I was aching with longing, my body quivering as he moved his lips down my neck to my breasts, the nipples hard with longing.

He unbuttoned my shirt and he gently worked it down my arms, his lips kissing my skin as he did so. I shut my eyes, my body unable to resist the sensations he aroused in me as his lips moved over my skin, nuzzling my breasts through the soft fabric of my bra.

I groaned and tried to lie still, but then he was slowly taking my bra off and his lips were at my naked breasts, licking and kissing them. His tongue, so warm and soft, lapped at my hard breasts, making me ache with longing. I groaned as he gently stroked my nipples, then slowly moved down, kissing my body as he went.

I was unable to move as he moved lower, unbuttoning my trousers and drawing them down my legs with a soft, fluid movement. I was naked on the bed now, except for my underwear, which he gently removed, dragging my panties down until I helped to work them off, leaving me naked in front of him.

He kissed my neck, then his hand moved between my thighs, gently stroking the sensitive places. I lay back, feeling him touch me, and gasped aloud as his finger found my clit. I felt my body tighten as he gently stroked there; so gently that it made my nerves ache and made me long for more and more.

I pushed against him as he touched me, encouraging him. He stroked me again, a little harder this time, and I cried aloud as he moved his finger harder and faster. I wanted him to never stop touching me, feeling him stroking my thick, wet folds as he moved his finger harder and faster and harder...

I cried out, unable to hold back any longer as my nerves raced with the sensations that swamped me. I lay back, gasping, unable to believe what had just happened. He was undressing now, and it sent a fresh wave of longing through me as he entered me.

I shut my eyes again, unable to resist as he drove into me. It was big and thick, and filled me. He thrust in again, and I cried out, feeling his fullness rubbing inside me, rubbing on all the places that made me long for him, that made me want him more and more.

He was moving faster, and I could sense that he was close to climax. I embraced him, drawing him against me as he moved, wanting more of him, wanting him inside me as he moved and moved and thrust.

I cried out as he gasped aloud, his body moving almost without his conscious mind, as if our two bodies knew what they were doing and we were connected in a way that made no sense except for the desire that raced through us.

He collapsed on me and I wrapped my arms around him, holding him. It had been fast, but intense, and I could feel fulfilment soaking through me, making me sleep.

He rolled over, held me and we lay, cheeks touching, skin wet, arms wrapped tight around each other.

Chapter 10: Christina

I woke up the next morning to the smell of toast. I sniffed, not quite able to believe what I was smelling. I rolled over, memory instantly telling me where I was. I was in Brett Caden's house.

I sat up in bed. It was soft and warm, the brown coverlet velvety-soft and pulled up around my shoulders. I looked around.

The bedroom was white-painted, I saw now, with white curtains and a thin dark line about the wall as an accent color – everything either white or chocolaty-dark. I looked at our clothes, strewn on the bed, on the floor and bedside-chair, and flushed scarlet.

Memories of the night – so passionate and intense – washed through me. I grinned.

My stomach growled as I got out of bed. I realized we hadn't eaten anything – we had slept, and kissed, and slept again. I tiptoed to the shower. I was sure he wouldn't mind if I had a shower before I went. I wondered what the time was and whether we were going to make it in time for work without notice.

I showered, hurrying to find my clothes. My underwear was discarded on the mat, my trousers left in one corner. I went red, remembering last night and how we had undressed with such urgency.

I dressed and tiptoed out of the room. I looked over and watched Brett Caden, CEO of one of the biggest magazine publication companies, carefully buttering whole wheat bread.

He seemed not to know I was there, but I bumped against the doorframe as I tiptoed forward.

"I made toast," he said, his voice gentle. "I also have muesli if you would prefer. And nice milk. I always try to get the best products I can around here."

"Sounds good," I said. Tiptoeing across the thick carpet, I joined him in the kitchen. It was a masterpiece of black countertops and dark tiles. I loved it. I rested a hand on his arm. He looked up at me.

I felt my body tingle as he rested a hand on my shoulder. I could see longing in his eyes and my heart thudded as he stroked my hair.

"We should eat," he said. "You didn't eat anything last night. I'm worried about you."

I chuckled. "You didn't, either."

"I did sneak in here and eat some bread," he said with a grin, cheeks red. "Then I got back in beside you – I thought you should eat something to, but I didn't think it would be right to wake you."

I smiled. "I slept so well."

"Me, too."

I felt my heart tug, and this time it wasn't just longing, but something much deeper. He looked so young, his shirt unbuttoned, his smile warm below messy hair. I wondered if he'd showered yet. I went to join him at the table.

"So," he said, passing me a plate with some slices of toast on it. The toast was crisp and well-buttered, the butter spread across it properly, right up to the edges. I bit into a piece, and he chuckled. "I hope you're going to have muesli as well...you didn't have dinner and you need lots of energy."

I nodded. "Sounds good."

I had to admit I was hungry. I grinned to myself. I had never actually experienced anything like this before – the feeling of intense joy and fulfilment that I felt, just being with him.

"So," he said, standing and fetching something from the sideboard. "I hope that you are going to discuss something with your boss today."

I felt my brow raise. "I don't want to think about work," I said.

He chuckled. "No. I don't blame you. You're right. We shouldn't be talking about work."

He looked down, and I could see his cheeks reddening. He was so awkward this morning. I wanted to kiss him. I felt his hand move towards mine and I gently took it, my fingers tight on his.

"You have helped me so much," I began carefully. He shook his head.

"You have nothing to thank me for. I thank you," he said gently.

I looked into his eyes and then felt my own cheeks red with a flush as he tenderly stroked my hair back behind one ear. I felt that same ache in my heart.

We ate breakfast in silence.

I washed the dishes after we had finished, and I heard him go through to the bedroom. I thought he was going to shower – I didn't think he had yet. It was so sweet of him to make breakfast first, I thought. I rinsed the bowls and cups, listening to the sounds of him in the shower.

I smiled to myself. I had never actually felt like this about anyone. I couldn't quite believe that I really felt this way for him – but, then, I had seen another side of him when he comforted me so sweetly; though I thought that I had seen that side before, when we had talked in the hallway, for example.

I just hadn't acknowledged its truth.

I dried my hands on the towel. It was eight a.m. and, depending on the traffic, we would definitely make it on time. He came out of the bedroom. He was wearing casual trousers and a white shirt, a blazer thrown casually over his shoulder in a black that matched the trousers. I felt my body light up.

"Come on," he said. "Let's go to work."

I felt my heart thump as I followed him down the stairs. I didn't know what our colleagues would think if they saw us arrive together. He seemed unworried, but I couldn't help expressing some doubts.

"What will everyone think?" I asked.

He frowned. "What do you think they'll think?" He shrugged. "They can speculate as much as they want, about us."

I went red. "Brett," I said. I felt my throat tighten. "I don't want people to say things about us. I don't want to think of what the people in the office would say if they thought I'd...done that."

He looked confused. "Well, okay. But I am not letting you walk to work. At least let me take you as far as the store. Just that."

"Okay," I said. I took a deep breath. I wasn't sure about anything anymore. I didn't know how I felt, how he felt, or what anyone would think. I needed to think clearly. I followed him down the stairs to his car. I got in, feeling uncomfortable.

"We'll be there early," he said, looking at the clock. It was quarter past eight. I frowned. We would probably need more time, if the traffic was bad. As it happened, though, he was right. It was much clearer than it usually was when I drove to work.

We didn't say much as we drove. I commented on the traffic. He explained that it had cleared. We drove through the town. On the one hand, I was wishing we would hurry, so that none of our colleagues would see us in the car. But also, I liked it in here. I liked the scent of his cologne, his voice as he talked. I liked being here with him.

I watched the downtown area come into sight. We had been in the car for a few minutes, but I felt like he was deliberately not making conversation and so I stayed still, not wanting to disturb him or to say or do anything that he wouldn't be comfortable with. I sensed that he didn't want to talk for some or other reason.

We drove along through the street. I could see the store now – the shopping mall that was just round the corner from the big high-rise where we worked. I felt my heart thump and glanced over the street as the light changed. I didn't know how we were going to do this, but this seemed like a good chance.

"Shall I get out?" I asked.

He looked across at me. It was so hard to read his expression. It could have been neutral, but there was a storm in his dark eyes, a sense of so many emotions I couldn't discern.

He nodded. "If you like. I'll unlock it." He clicked a button and my door unlocked. I stepped out and into the street. I waved at him.

"See you at work," I called.

He nodded, raising a hand. I wished I could understand the secrets in those dark eyes. They were too complex for me to read.

I wished I could understand what they meant.

I walked down the street, the image of his face at the forefront of my mind, again and again, no matter how much I tried to blank it out. I walked up the stairs and greeted the secretary at the front desk woodenly as I went through to sit at the desk in my office.

I couldn't believe that I was sitting here, in my office, as though yesterday had been an ordinary day at the office.

My eyes scanned down the screen. I couldn't recall half the stuff I wrote yesterday. Some of it made sense. It was good. I read through my own work, feeling impressed. I had gotten about a quarter of the way through, which meant that if I really worked hard today, I could get it done by the end of the workday.

I bent over my keyboard and started work slowly.

I tried to focus, but the figures swam in front of my eyes and I kept on thinking of Brett and me. I recalled his face close to mine, his eyes shut, the sound of how he spoke; so soft and low, his voice loving as he talked to me.

I took a deep breath. He had been so caring last night! I would never have imagined him capable of such sweetness. But then, I would never have imagined what had happened.

I focused on the screen, trying to think about work. Images of Brett filled my mind – his gorgeous body, his handsome mouth. I tried so hard to think about values and investments and I think, to some extent, I managed.

By the time it was lunchtime, my focus was absolute. I had been working solidly for about two hours when I heard someone coughing. I looked up to find my boss in the doorway. I tensed.

"How is it, Christina?"

"It's fine," I said. I looked at him wearily. I hoped he could see how exhausted I was. I thought he looked uncomfortable, and I was quite pleased about that.

"Look, I know it's a lot of work," he said carefully. "I wouldn't have entrusted it to anybody else."

"Yeah," I said. I hoped he could hear the anger in my voice. "I know."

He had threatened me, or I wouldn't have agreed to do this. And I wanted him to know that I hadn't forgiven him for it, and that I was unlikely to. I was angry.

"Christina, let me know if you need anything, okay?" he said.

"Yeah," I said.

I didn't say anything else, but went across the room to get one of my files out of the cupboard. Somewhere in there, I had written down my part of the calculations. Burgess left, and I got on with my work.

I worked through lunchtime, and by two o' clock I was lightheaded with hunger. I went wandering out of my office and into the coffee-room. There was a fridge there and a machine with candy. I really needed something to eat – anything, really. I just needed to raise my blood sugar before I fell over.

"Christina!" Neela greeted me as I came out of the coffee-room, a sandwich in my hand. "Hey! How're you?"

"I'm fine," I said. I swallowed a bite of my sandwich. "I'm just working quite hard today."

"Yeah, okay," Neela nodded. Then she looked at me carefully. "Christina? Something's made you smile."

"What?" I blushed. Was it that obvious? I might have a hectic workload, but I had been smiling more today than I think I had smiled in a week before today. I just hadn't known that it was so apparent.

"Nothing...just that you look different," Neela said. "Happier. I guess maybe I'm just imagining it, seeing as you say that you're really working."

"Well, I am happy," I said carefully. "No reason someone can't work hard and be happy, is there?"

Neela frowned at me. She smiled, a slow smile that suggested that even if I was crazy she still loved me. She shrugged. "Well, no, I guess not," she said. "You look after yourself though, Christina."

"I will," I said. I gestured with the sandwich, the drooping lettuce hanging out of the sides unconvincingly. I suppose, as lunches go, it didn't exactly look like I was practicing self-care.

"I'll see you later," Neela called over her shoulder as she went up the hallway. She ignored the sandwich; a sensible course of action, I thought. "I'll be passing this way in a couple of hours to deliver some stuff to the technical guys." She gestured to some forms in her hand.

I nodded to her. "I will hopefully be finished by the end of today, and then maybe we can talk properly," I promised. At least, I would try and be finished by then. I had no idea if I would actually manage it, and, by this stage, I didn't really feel any responsibility to do so.

"Awesome. Can't wait!"

I nodded and she hurried off, going back up the hallway to her own office at the end of the corridor. I went in and sat down at my desk. I was exhausted. I had decided that I wasn't going to focus on getting it done, but instead I was going to focus on doing my best.

I opened the spreadsheet and moved to the next column. I was explaining things one column at a time, more or less. I opened the document where I was writing the report and set to work. I only had a few more hours and I reckoned I was slightly more than halfway. Not too bad. Having spoken to Neela had raised my spirits a bit, I had to admit – to say nothing of what the previous night had done, despite being confusing.

I tried to focus on numbers and letters when all I could think about was Brett, and smile as I thought about how obvious it had been to Neela that I had a good time last night.

Chapter 11: Christina

I finished the report just on time on Friday evening. I went to Burgess's office to give it to him, my back stiff and my face schooled to calm. I was angry with him, but I couldn't be that angry, since, after all, something really good had come out of that night.

"Here," I said. "The report. I sent you a copy, but here is a hard copy too." I put the freshly-printed sheets down on his desk. He raised a brow.

"Thanks, Christina. That was fast. I really owe you one." He sounded sincere. He was already leafing through the pages, his brows raising as he looked at the columns of figures, the long explanations, the charts I'd made.

"Yes," I said lightly. "That's true. I'll think of something."

Burgess raised a brow. "That surprises me, Christina." His eyes were wide and he looked a little affronted, as if I'd insulted him.

I felt a wash of annoyance at that. Had he really been planning to take advantage of my good nature? I was taking no more than my due, claiming a favor from him, but he didn't expect that. He expected me to simply smile and say thank you and go back to my office. I put my head on one side.

"I am full of surprises, Mr. Burgess. Have a good weekend."

I walked out of his office, leaving him looking after me with a confused expression. I couldn't help a chuckle. He was well and truly flummoxed by all that had changed about me. Leaning back in my office chair, I contemplated that. I was well and truly confused, too. I thought back over the events of yesterday night, my mouth lifting with a smile.

I had never felt like that before. In my previous relationships, I had never felt that connection, that wonderful feeling that I'd had last night that I couldn't quite explain. I opened my eyes again, hastily sitting up as I heard someone going down the hallway.

"Good night, Christina. Have a good weekend."

I smiled at the secretary from our department. "Thanks. You too."

She waved and walked away, her shoes making a thump on the carpeting as she went down towards the stairs. I stood, sleepily gathering my things and packing them away. I was lost in a haze of thoughts. I didn't know what would happen from now, but I weirdly wasn't worried about it. A strange calmness had settled on my heart. I felt that whatever was going to happen, it was bound to be good.

I hadn't really put any thought into what I expected to happen – if Brett talked to me, good; if he just forgot about it, I reckoned that would also be fine. After all, we were adults and I had no idea what he was really like – if he chose to act like I was just his senior executive, I felt that was for the best as well.

"Weird," I said aloud to myself. I had never felt like that before. My whole life had been shaped by the fears of my childhood – my fear that my dad would finally lose it and hurt me, my fear that we'd have no home and be out on the street. It was only when Uncle Hal had paid for me to go away to high school that I'd had even an inkling of relief, and even then I'd been terrified my dad would show up and find me. It was strange – so strange –without constant fear. I realized that yesterday night had been the first time someone had held me when I was frightened, had comforted me and told me I was safe and it was okay.

I picked up my handbag and went to the door. It was both wonderful and strange to be without constant fear – I felt a bit like I imagine a butterfly would. Discovering you have wings can be scary, and sometimes you think it was safer and more comfortable without them.

I was walking across to the printing-room to pick up some last documents when someone walked in, quite silently.

"Christina?"

I turned. I would recognize that voice anywhere. I found myself looking at Brett. He smiled, a slow, shy smile; one lip quirked downwards in what I was starting to learn was his embarrassed grin.

"Brett," I said. I spoke softly, just in case any of the employees in the corridor were still here. It was six o' clock, so I doubted it, but it was better to be safe. "What are you doing here?"

He smiled. "I wanted to check on you. How are you? Did you get that work finished?"

"Yes," I said. I felt my stomach tense with nerves and excitement. Just being with him felt like a wash of cool seawater across my body – exciting.

"Good," he said. He frowned. Came to stand a little closer. The tension – the sense of waiting – was so strong I could have reached out and touched it like the string on a guitar. "You feel okay this morning?"

"Yeah," I said. I frowned up at him, feeling a grin tug my own lips. "I feel good, actually."

He smiled and the brightness in his eyes showed that he knew exactly what I meant. "Good," he said. "I slept beautifully."

"Same."

We grinned at each other, delighted to be sharing a secret. I felt my tummy tingle as he stepped closer. I ached for him, wanting his lips on mine, his touch on my skin, his hands on my waist as he drew me toward him. I knew it was dangerous – here in the printing-room, anybody could see us. He rested a hand on my shoulder, gently.

"Christina," he murmured. "What are you doing this weekend?"

"Um..." I wet my lips, heart thumping. If I had expected him to say anything, the last thing I'd expected was that! He raised a brow, and I tried to get my thoughts into some kind of order where I could actually answer him. "Um, nothing," I said honestly.

He grinned. "No meetings to prepare for?"

"Um, not really," I said. My heart was beating crazily fast, my face flushed, my body hot. I tried to control my breathing. "I was just planning to relax and maybe prepare something for the budget meeting next week..." I gasped as he rested his hands on my shoulders, drawing me close.

"Well, then," he said, looking into my eyes, his own eyes sparkling with interest. "If I may, I would like to visit you. Shall we say ten tomorrow morning?"

"Um, yeah," I said. I was too shocked to think of anything else to say. Brett wanted to visit me? At my apartment? I tried to breathe.

"Great," he said. He stepped closer, so close that his body was pressed to mine. Then, just as quickly, he stepped away. "Well, then. I'll see you then. Will you text the details?"

"Um, sure."

I waited until he had gone until I let out a long, slow breath. My brain was racing and I could hardly think.

I fetched the documents from the printer and went down to my car. I couldn't believe it. I was going to see Brett tomorrow.

I drove back to my apartment and the first thing I did – after making myself some dinner, just some pasta to reheat – after putting on the washing-machine, was to clean. I tidied up the sitting-room, packed away clothes that had been lying around waiting to be put away, and swept the rooms. Then I showered and collapsed gratefully into bed for an early night.

Chapter 12: Christina

I woke up early the next morning, stretching and feeling rested. I went to the shower and turned it on, feeling dreamy and happy. I was going to see Brett. I was thinking of him as I dried my hair and checked my reflection in the mirror carefully. My long oval face looked back at me, eyes bright and full of life. I brushed my hair until it was shiny, then went through to choose some clothes.

I settled on a good pair of jeans and a silky blouse. The pale lilac color brought out the brown of my eyes, I thought, and the fabric felt nice on my skin. I added a bit of makeup – just the barest touch of blush and mascara, just to make me look awake and alert. Then I went down to the kitchen for breakfast.

I sat there eating my cereal, thinking about just how surreal this was. I had got up this morning to get ready to see Brett Caden. For a date. I grinned to myself. How weird was that? I would never have imagined that we could even get along professionally.

I was washing the dishes when I heard someone ring the bell. I jumped, heart thudding. It was him! I ran to the intercom and pressed the button.

"Good morning?"

"Christina! It's me! Will you unlock for me?"

"Sure," I said. I pressed the button and felt my heart race with excitement. I looked around the room, thinking that maybe I should have cleaned thoroughly, that the couch probably could have done with a dust-off and that the corners were cobwebby.

"Hello?" Someone called, tapping lightly on the door.

I ran to the door and opened it. I stared.

Brett grinned at me shyly. His hair was brushed beautifully, and he wore a casual button-down shirt and jeans. I had never seen him dressed like that and I was amazed by the new side of him it brought out. He looked so sexy, and yet oddly approachable. Masculine, too –

in a sort of hard way. I felt my stomach tighten with longing and I just wanted him so much then.

"So," he said, his shy grin expanding as he looked around and back to me. "Good morning. This is good." He gestured at the apartment and at me, awkwardly. "Being here, like this."

I felt my own shy grin bloom on my lips. "Um, yeah," I said. My stomach was tingling like I'd swallowed all the bubbly water on the planet. I grinned at him, unable to hide how joyful I felt to see him. "It's good."

"So," he said again, looking around. "This is your apartment. It's nice."

"It is," I said. I tried to remember manners. "Would you like to sit down?"

We were talking to each other so desperately shyly, like two schoolkids on a first date, scared to say the wrong thing and make a fool of ourselves, yet thrilled to be close. It was the most tender, beautiful feeling! I felt myself grin.

"Oh. Yeah," he said. He grinned back at me, looking twenty years younger. He suddenly seemed an awkward teenager and I felt my heart flood with tenderness.

"I'll make coffee. You drink coffee, yes?" I asked.

He nodded. "Yeah. Please. Have you got water?" he asked. "I mean, I'm sure you've got water." He chuckled, nervously. "What am I thinking?"

"Yeah, I have water. Would you like to drink some?" I asked. He chuckled.

"Thanks. That'd be great. It was a long drive."

"I guess it must have been," I said. I could vaguely recall which neighborhood his apartment was in, enough to recall it was fairly far away from mine. I made the coffee and looked around for cups. I like strong coffee, and I had no idea what he liked.

"Thanks," he said as I brought out to small cups of black coffee. I had poured milk into a measuring jug – I didn't have a milk-jug, so I had to improvise – and brought some sugar out. He sipped his coffee without either. I grinned.

"You also drink it black."

"Absolutely. It's nice to feel that tingle in your toes."

I laughed. "I know what you mean."

I looked across at him, feeling myself relax. He was grinning easily, and it was weird how comfortable I felt. It was at once so strange to have him here, and entirely normal, like we always sat here and talked on Saturday mornings.

"About Thursday night," Brett said. He looked at me, cheeks red.

"What about it?" I asked. I tried to sound casual, but my heart was racing, my body on fire. I didn't know what he would say, so I waited to see.

"I hope you...I mean...I hope that you want to do that again?"

I stared at him. My heart flooded with warmth. I would never have expected him to say something like that! I smiled at him, not knowing quite what to say. I felt elated.

"Sure," I said.

"Sure?" He was staring at me now, brown eyes wide, a surprised grin on his face. I had to chuckle.

"Brett!" I said, grinning back at him. "I think it must have been pretty clear I liked it. And you wouldn't be here if I had been mad about it."

"No," he agreed. He was flushed red and I wondered if he was thinking about what we had done the previous night and how wonderful it had been. I certainly was and I looked away, embarrassed, lest he could guess my thoughts.

We sat together silently for a while in the still warmth of the morning.

"So," he said, sipping his coffee. "How do you like it here?" He looked up at me shyly, eyes wide with inquiry.

"You mean, this apartment?" I asked.

"Yeah," he said. "This apartment, this city, this work...you know. It's weird, how I feel I know you, even though we haven't talked much."

"I know what you mean."

We smiled shyly. I cleared my throat.

"I came here from Connecticut five years ago. I had my first job there and I studied there," I said. I left out the details – that I had worked super-hard at college; hard enough to get a paying internship that helped to pay off some of my college debt. That I had grown up in the poorest part of town and I had been no stranger to hunger and need.

"Wow. Long way from home," he said, raising one brow.

"I guess." I grinned. "That's kind of what was so encouraging when the job came up."

I hadn't meant that to come out, but it had – somehow I almost wanted to share my past with him.

"Oh. Yeah." He nodded, and I could see that he felt awkward, as if he'd raised a bad topic. I wanted him to feel at ease and I shifted in my seat, trying to think of something I could do to make him chill out. He beat me to it with a question. "So, what made you study finance?"

I shrugged, glad for the change of subject. "I don't know. I guess I always liked it. Finance is like a separate world – it makes sense in a way that society doesn't. Like, with finance, there are equations and laws and it all follows its own rules. Yeah, it sometimes looks like there are no rules, but it's a system and in some ways it's not difficult to follow. Not like people."

He nodded, a frown on his brow. "Yeah," he said. "I get that. People can be confusing sometimes, I guess."

We smiled at each other and I felt like he understood what I meant, like he got it, at least superficially. I wondered about his own story –

why he had started a publishing company for magazines, and how he'd got so successful so quickly. I was about to ask him when he cleared his throat.

"So, what do you like most about being here?" he asked.

"You mean, this city?"

"Like, right here," he said, gesturing at the room. "Your apartment."

"I chose it for how it looks – I really like beautiful things – but I guess I like most being able to sit in front of that window at night. The way the little lights in all the windows twinkle in the dark. It seems friendly and close, and safe."

I hadn't realized how much emotion was in my voice. I looked up to see him smiling at me. "That is so great," he said sincerely. "You know, you are making me like the city."

I giggled.

"You are a lovely person, Christina."

I felt my throat tighten. I didn't think anyone had ever said that. The closest anyone had come to saying that to me was Neela, and even she had never said it freely. I took a deep breath, my heart responding to his soft touch on my hands, and to the kindness in his eyes.

"Thank you," I said. "And you are too."

He looked away, a small smile on his lips. "I don't know," he said awkwardly. "But thanks."

I felt my own heart twist and I squeezed his fingers. "Yes, you are."

He looked into my eyes and then, without any discussion, he stood and came and sat beside me. His eyes were soft on mine.

"Christina," he said shyly. "I hope you know that I want you."

"You mean now?" I asked, a tingle of longing creeping up my spine, my heart thudding in my chest.

His voice was soft. "Yes."

I felt my body heat up instantly. He rested his hand on my shoulder, his face close to mine. I felt his hand move to the back of my neck as he drew me closer.

"I hope you know that I have always wanted you," he whispered. "Because I have, and it sure makes it impossible to resist you now." His breath was tight in his throat and I felt my own body warm up as his lips touched mine.

I let my lips part under his and he gently pushed me back onto the couch. His body, so firm and muscled, was hard on mine as he kissed me, his knee moving between mine.

I gasped and drew him closer, and our kiss was urgent with longing. His hands were on my back, running up along my waist. I wrapped my arms around him, my fingers stroking his back as he kissed me. He moved, sitting up.

"Shall we go to your room?"

I nodded. "Yes," I whispered.

I sat up and ran a hand through my hair, tucking it back behind my ears. I stood and went breathlessly to my bedroom, opening the door. The bed was made, and I'd put away my clothes. He looked around a moment, taking in the window with the lacey curtain, and the wardrobe.

"Christina," he murmured.

He buried his face in my neck and I held him close, my body pressed to his. Suddenly, I wanted to go slowly, to savor his body and have him savor mine. I ran my hands down his ribs, sliding them up under his shirt, feeling his thick muscles under my skin.

He seemed to understand, because his lips went from my mouth and down, pushing me back gently onto the bed so he could kiss my breasts. I shut my eyes, letting him gently, so gently, unbutton my top and reach for my breasts.

He squeezed them gently, touching them through the fabric of my bra. I shifted on the bed, letting him reach the clasp and he undid it, then bent and put his mouth to my breast.

I gasped, as his tongue played gently over it, making me cry out. My nipple throbbed and he sucked it and I could feel the sensation running from my breasts to my stomach.

He moved lower, making a trail of kisses down my tummy and stopping at my trousers. Gently, he unbuttoned them, looking at my eyes. I grinned, letting him know I wasn't scared.

He drew my trousers down my legs, then reached up and carefully removed my panties, leaving me unclothed. He ran a hand up, parting my legs, and his fingers stroked my warm folds. I shut my eyes, gasping, as he buried his face in them. His tongue was warm and questing, seeking out the nodule between and I tried to control my gasps as he gently bit and teased it with his tongue.

I couldn't lie still, my body pushing against him, wanting him and wanting more, and more...He licked me and I cried out, feeling my climax wash through me, way earlier than anticipated.

He looked up, and his eyes shone, like he thought he'd done something clever. I had to smile. He was clearly so pleased with himself and I reached for him, drawing him up the bed. I ran my hand down his chest, moving to unzip his trousers.

He watched me and I wanted to laugh as he grinned, helping me undo them. I pulled them awkwardly down his muscled thighs. I hastily undid his shirt, and he helpfully withdrew his arms from the sleeves, leaving himself clad only in his boxers. I pulled them off, unable to stop myself staring admiringly at his manhood, but he blushed and I felt myself smile as I looked away.

I reached for it, taking it in my fingers and then in my mouth. He gasped and tensed as I sucked. I could feel his body responding and I wasn't sure what he wanted, but he gently gripped my arm, drawing me up to beside him.

"I want to be inside," he said.

I nodded and let him roll me onto my back and watched him kneel between my legs, his own face frowning in concentration as he rubbed himself against me, slipping in the wetness on my legs. I parted my thighs and he slid into me. I cried out at the fullness.

He was big, but just right. He rubbed against the special spots inside me and I could feel my longing grow as he drew out and pushed in again. He was gasping, and I was gasping too, my legs gripping him as he moved into me, wanting more of him as he thrust and gasped and thrust.

He knelt up, altering the angle of his thrusting and I cried aloud, unable to contain the sensations that were running through my body, making me light up inside, making my body focus only on itself, my nerves and muscles tingling and throbbing as he pushed into me again and again and again.

He was moving faster, and I could feel how tense he was, and I was just as tense, my arms stiff and my legs wrapped around him as he plunged, moving faster and faster.

I cried out for a second time, unable to hold back, and he cried out too, then rested on top of me. I wrapped my arms around him, holding him close, his body weight feeling good as he lay there, my body fully and completely relaxed below him as we lay together, arms wrapped around each other.

I was almost asleep, but he rolled off me and gently drew the blankets up. He lay beside me, his arms around me, and I rested my head beside his on the pillow. I held him close, my body feeling better than if I'd slept for a year.

He rolled onto his side, and I rolled so that his arms wrapped me close, drawing my chest against him, our bodies so close that even the sheet seemed thick in comparison to the space between us. He was sleeping, and my own breath started to match the rhythm of his as I drifted off to sleep.

I held him and felt better than I could ever remember feeling before.

Chapter 13: Brett

I looked at Christina who was lying with her head on the pillow, her eyes shut. She had her one arm out of the blanket, long and pale on the dark cover, her beautiful skin as soft as petals in the gentle light. I resisted the urge to stroke her long hair, to kiss my way up that long arm to her neck and bury my face in its scent. Her eyelashes rested on her soft cheek and I watched her lip tremble as she breathed.

She was so beautiful, lying there, so tender. I wanted to kiss her, but I also wanted her to sleep. I watched her for a moment, then rolled over to sit up.

She stirred, breathing in slowly, and I wished I hadn't disturbed her, but then her dark eyes widened. I found myself looking into her eyes. She was frowning for a moment, but then she saw me and smiled. I bent and touched her cheek.

"Good afternoon," I said.

She grinned and laced her fingers through mine. I felt my heart melt. I had always wanted her, but the feeling in my heart was one of immense warmth, beyond the longing I had felt before.

"Hello, Brett," she said.

I bent and kissed her. She smiled and wrapped her arms around me, drawing me against her. I held her close, my body aroused, but wanting not to scare her, or do anything to disrupt her. She held me and I held her, my fingers in her hair.

She rolled onto her back and I sat up, looking down at her. She was smiling, dark eyes shining.

"Did you have a good sleep?" I asked.

She nodded and rolled over, and I gasped as she reached for me, drawing me against her. My lips parted for her kiss and I found myself aching with longing. I pushed her back onto the bed and ran my hand down her leg.

We made love again, both of us gripped with an urgency of longing I hadn't expected. I had thought that I wouldn't be ready again for another hour or two, but I found myself coming with the same sheer longing as before.

She cried out and held me and I lay down beside her, soaked with sweat. I grinned.

"Whew," I said. "I didn't think that would happen…"

She giggled, looking into my eyes. I loved the sound of her laughter. I would do anything to make her laugh, I thought. "Yeah, me too."

We lay there together and I felt my heart beating more-slowly. I drew a long breath and sat.

"I guess we should wash up," I said. She grinned and nodded.

"Yes. Let's go and get ourselves washed off. I wonder how late it is?"

I shrugged. "I guess it must be lunchtime, or around lunchtime."

"Yeah," she said.

We looked at each other, and I felt oddly shy. We had just spent the whole morning in bed, and I was glowing with the sweet release of that.

"So," I said, as I got out of bed and went to the bathroom. "What would you usually do?"

"You mean, on weekends?" she asked. She was standing in the doorway of the bathroom, and I could feel the way her eyes moved up and down across my skin, but oddly I felt proud, not shy. I could see approval in her gaze and it made me feel appreciated. I glowed.

"Yeah," I said, turning on the shower. It was cold, and I waited for a moment or two before getting in. She giggled as I let out a hiss, feeling the surprising shock of coldness on my skin.

"Well," she said, watching as I took shower-gel and started washing myself. "I would have eaten by now, but let me shower first, seeing as I'm used to waiting a good long time for the heated water."

I grimaced as I stepped back, realizing now that it might take some time.

"And later I'd do some working out, and just spend an hour or two reading and relaxing." She replied, stepping out of the water. Her body was damp and lovely and I ached to draw her against me and kiss the water from her skin.

"Good idea," I said, struggling to resist the temptation to kiss her. I let her get out of the shower and wrap a towel around herself, her gorgeous body covered with its warm softness. I went back into the cubicle. The water was bearable, and I reached for the shower-gel again. "I think I should add that to my mornings. It's a good way to deal with stress."

"Yeah," she agreed. She grinned at me as I reached for the towel. I have always been fast and efficient with stuff like showering. I dried myself off and went through to the bedroom, where she was dressing, taking an opportunity to stare at her nakedness. She went pink and reached for her underwear. I watched her step into it, my longing hard to fight – but if I didn't, we'd never get out of bed. "It's important to de-stress once a week."

"I try to jog on the weekend," I said. "But usually, I spend my morning with friends. Which maybe isn't the best idea, since I never really take time for myself."

"That's not good," she said.

"No, it isn't," I agreed.

I was trying to talk, but really I was distracted. Her body was so beautiful, the last traces of damp still running down her back, shining on her generous curves, and I was mesmerized by her.

I was still staring at her when she turned around.

"Shall we have lunch?" she asked. Her smile teased me, as if she knew that I was longing for her.

I shrugged and nodded. "Do you have stuff to cook?" I asked her. I tried to drag my mind away from how beautiful she was, her wet hair clinging to her pale skin, but I couldn't reasonably expect the mundane topic like grocery-shopping to do the trick, really.

"Well, yeah, I guess."

"What would you normally have?" I asked. She was patting her hair dry now, her lips parted as she drew a breath, and I felt my jaw clench, trying to control myself. I couldn't very well drag her back to bed, not after just rising.

"Something warm," she said, gesturing at the kitchen. "Stew, maybe. And some nice bread. I always buy that good one from the bakery on the corner. It isn't stuffed full of chemicals, so it actually goes stale. I prefer that...Bread isn't supposed to last a week."

I laughed. I had never encountered this side of her – the down-to-earth side. At meetings, I saw how ruthlessly practical she was, how efficient. But the side that was freaked out by preservatives in loaves was a new one. I wanted to know everything about her, I thought with a grin.

"That's right," I agreed. "Bread isn't supposed to last a week. Remember when we were kids? You could still get normal bread then." I chuckled.

"Yes," she said softly. Again, I detected tension in her and I looked around, seeking to change the subject. The past was clearly not a good subject for her and it wasn't worth scaring her right now.

"You have lots of stuff in this cupboard," I said, opening one above the dishwasher. She shrugged.

"Yeah, I do. That's the wrong one. Pasta and other stuff for lunch is in here."

I nodded, letting her direct me about the kitchen. We made a stew with vegetables, and cooked some rice. I felt my stomach twist with hunger. I was really hungry.

We set about making the stew together. It felt odd, working with her – as if we were used to working with each other. Which, I supposed, we were – after all, we were colleagues and we saw each other at work every other week. We just hadn't cooked stew before. The thought made me grin. Here I was, cooking stew with the sexiest finance exec in the world.

Weirdly, it didn't feel strange at all. It just felt wonderful.

"What was the cuisine like, in your hometown?" I asked her. I wanted to find out stuff about her, but at the same time I didn't want to risk just asking her directly. She was clearly not comfortable with stuff in her past and I didn't know how traumatic it was. I decided to go carefully.

She shrugged. "No idea, really. I guess your usual western US stuff, for the most part. I don't know. I didn't really eat out." She looked down at the cutting-board, where she was busy chopping onions for the stew.

"I see," I said. "At college, you must have eaten out sometimes?"

She raised a brow. "Not really. I was in a rented apartment shared between three of us. We mostly cooked for each other. I guess I was lucky to survive the cooking."

I chuckled. "Well, you clearly learned to cook," I said. I had sampled the stew that was nicely-flavored, rich and creamy. I was sure I was going to enjoy the meal a great deal. She smiled.

"I guess I had to learn," she said. "It was pretty tricky, since the ingredients were limited to whatever anyone had remembered to buy – and of course, what was on offer – but in a way that was a nice way to learn – basically it was an achievement if it didn't kill people."

I laughed loudly. She had such a good humor, and that was something that I hadn't known before. She was usually serious in our meetings, and I'd never seen her like this.

We went to sit down to eat the stew and some slices of toast I'd buttered. I helped myself to more stew, enjoying the texture.

"You stayed in rented accommodation?" I asked, wanting to know more. I recalled my own study years – I had been in residence for all three, and never had to cook anything in all that time. I had never really thought of myself as privileged, but I was starting to see how different others' experiences were from my own.

She nodded, answering my question. "Yeah, I did. With one girl and one guy who studied politics with me. That was my other major – Economics, and political science. I loved the first major...not too sure why I did the second one."

"No, me neither," I said with a grin. "If the economy is chaotic, I can't imagine how chaotic politics is."

She laughed. "I like that," she said.

I blushed. "Thanks," I said. I stretched my legs out under the table. "I guess I never really had to put much thought into my majors. Business science was what I wanted to do."

She smiled at me. "You were pretty decisive, then."

I chuckled. "I guess so." It had been easy for me because I knew what I wanted. I had wanted to become inordinately wealthy, and I had. That had been my only real goal. I wondered about that now, and about why that had been so important to me.

Christina gave me a fond look. "Well, I'm not sorry that you chose to own a big company...It made it a lot more likely that we would meet each other. After all, we're both in finance, more or less, now."

I felt my heart melt. She really valued having met me. I reached across to her hand and rested mine on it. "I think that's the sweetest thing I ever heard," I said sincerely. I held her hand, feeling the softness of her skin under my palms and the slight warmth of them.

She smiled at me. "You're sweet too."

We both grinned and I leaned over the table and planted a kiss on her shoulder. She touched my hair and the warmth in her eyes made me smile.

Chapter 14: Christina

I looked out of the window. I couldn't quite believe it. It was Sunday morning and I was waiting for Brett to come and fetch me. He had said he would come by after breakfast. I was thinking of him, still amazed about what had happened and how he felt.

We had such a lovely day together the previous day – he'd left at two o' clock, and promised to return to see me the next morning. I stared out over the city – for once, the road was quiet, only the odd car moving up the asphalt, the sound of the exhaust lost over the long distance up. Pale white clouds floated over the skyline; the sky touched with yellow. The scene was joyful, like the feeling in my heart.

"He really seems happy to be seeing me."

I smiled to myself. It was so weird. I would never have thought someone like Brett would like me – actually, I think the point was that I hadn't thought Brett would like anybody. He seemed so distant, so rude, if I was honest. And he'd not really spoken well to me in the past. I made a note to ask him about that.

I felt another grin wash over me. I was too happy to feel cross with him about how he had acted with me. I was too uplifted to really mind for now. I put away the dishes and went and checked what I looked like. I had chosen jeans and a coal-colored blouse in silk again – not quite black, but near enough to make my hair look brown and shiny. I had left it loose, liking the way it framed my oval face. I heard the doorbell and ran to answer.

"Hi, Christina!" Brett greeted me. I grinned and pressed the button, waiting for him to arrive.

He came upstairs and I grinned as he wrapped his arms around me. It felt safe and good to hold him and feel his strong arms tight around me. He was wearing a casual shirt and jeans and a coat and he smelled like cologne and I held him against me hard.

"Good morning," I whispered.

He grinned. "It is now. It is a warm day, you're right," he added when he stepped back. "A proper summery day. But you know...we can go to the park later." His eyes twinkled and he rested a hand on my shoulder in a way that left me no doubt as to what he meant.

I chuckled. "I also reckon it can wait. The park's not going anywhere, and there's something I want more." My cheeks went bright red. Was I really saying this?"

"Me, too."

We went to my room and made love. This time, we were slow and gentle and it felt beautiful but also natural, getting used to each other. I smiled up at him, my eyes focused on him from where I lay beside him. He was leaning on the headboard. He turned to look at me.

"I hope you know that you're gorgeous."

I smiled. "Not really...I suppose nobody knows what they look like."

He laughed. "I know I'm gorgeous."

I pushed him, a big grin spreading across my face. "Well! You are, but you seem to know that already." I smiled up at him playfully.

"So, you should too." He kissed me.

I wrapped my arms around him, holding him close as I thought about that. I hadn't been raised to think well of myself – anything but. The things that were said about me – loudly and forcefully – were anything but that I was gorgeous. I held tightly onto Brett, making my mind stay in this moment, where someone said lovely things, low-voiced.

"I'm glad you know you're gorgeous," I said to him, meaning it. It was good to know someone with self-esteem...it made it seem much more achievable. Not that I didn't know I had accomplished good things or that I wasn't aware of how I looked and how to make myself look even better – I just never really felt good about myself in spite of that.

He touched my hair gently. "Well, I was lucky to be raised to have good self-esteem. It's worth learning to love yourself, you know...it makes it a heck of a lot easier to love others, for a start."

I grinned. "I'll try," I promised.

"Good."

He kissed me and his hand snaked down to tickle me and I yelled and he laughed and then we were getting out of bed and going to the shower.

As soon as we were dressed, we went down to his car together. I got into the passenger seat, taking a moment to look at it. I had hardly noticed the details the previous night – my mind hadn't been on chrome and engines. I breathed in the scent of the interior as I sat down and looked around.

"Wow," I said. "Great wheels."

He blushed. "Thanks," he said. "I am happy with it. And knowing you like it makes it even better, to my mind."

I had to smile. "That's so sweet."

He chuckled. "Well, now that I've shown it off, I hope we can actually get somewhere and we don't just have to sit here in the parking-bay, breathing in the smell of the dashboard."

We both laughed. He turned the keys and I heard the engine purr to life. I couldn't help feeling a thrill of nervous energy race through me as we sped off towards the exit to the parking lot. We joined the traffic, blending seamlessly, and I watched the other cars go past, enjoying the wonderfully smooth engine.

The road from my house to the park was not too long, and soon we were looking for somewhere to park. I felt a wash of excitement as we found one and set off at a restful pace towards the pedestrian crossing.

"So," Brett said to me as we walked down the path. I looked over at him, admiring how his lithe, gorgeous body looked as he walked. He was more relaxed here, more direct. And it seemed as though his walk was more relaxed too; his arms swinging, a very slight favoring of the right leg that was somehow even more sexy than his businesslike walk. "So, do you usually come here on weekends? What does Christine typically do on weekends?" His eyes were bright and inquiring, mouth smiling.

I blushed. "Not much, actually." I felt a bit shy. I didn't really socialize much, outside Neela. I hadn't gotten into the habit of having groups of friends – when I was a kid, I had been on the edge of things.

"Do you have hobbies?" he wanted to know. I shrugged.

"Walking, reading...I love reading."

"Me too!" he exclaimed. "I don't really have a favorite genre – I read everything. Modern, classic, fiction, non-fiction...I just like books." He lifted a shoulder. He sounded pretty embarrassed too.

We walked down the path. The sunshine was pouring down onto the lawns, and kids were playing; chasing each other and practicing football moves. I slowed down as we passed an empty bench bathed in glorious warmth. Brett seemed to like the idea of sitting down too, and we settled down, looking out over the busy lawn.

"I like reading too," I said wistfully. Books had always been something of an escape for me. "In the world of a book, nobody could get me. I could float off into a place of castles and dragons and beauty, where my own world didn't exist for a while. It's like, books are their own worlds." I couldn't explain what I meant, but I felt very passionate about it.

Brett nodded. "Exactly! A book creates a world where anything is possible."

"Yes! I couldn't have said it so perfectly."

We smiled at each other. It was a conspiratorial smile, as if we shared some knowledge between us alone. I felt a strange warmth flood my heart. I had never actually met someone I connected to like this. In my past, I'd chosen men who treated me badly – I think that maybe I expected it and so I didn't object when they did. But now, I felt like I was talking to someone I liked talking to – someone I liked, in fact.

Brett was turning out to be a complex character, I thought – I had seen the businesslike, practical Brett and, just lately, I'd seen the passionate Brett. But it seemed that there were other facets to him that I wouldn't have guessed at – hidden depths and subtleties.

"It's pretty unusual, actually – being a reader," Brett said. He was looking at me with those beautiful brown eyes and my heart flipped over.

"I know," I said softly. "It's nice to find that out about you."

He grinned. "I reckon we have a lot to find out about each other."

That made me smile. We had already found out quite a lot, I wanted to say – but he was right. In terms of actual traits, I knew so little about him, and he of me.

I looked out over the lawn, my heart thumping. I could feel Brett's hand on mine as we sat there, just enjoying the busy noisiness of the park and our own shared calm. I watched two kids fighting over a football – a playful interaction that ended in them chasing each other around the field, laughing in high-pitched merriment. Brett was smiling.

"Typical boys," he grinned.

I nodded. I didn't really know, actually, now that I came to think about it. I hadn't any siblings and I hadn't really had any friends either, when I was that age. But they certainly seemed to be happy, healthy kids, and so I had to agree with him.

"Yeah," I said.

He chuckled as the kids kicked the ball together, laughing and squealing with excitement. He looked wistful, as if they reminded him of a time in his life.

I wondered about him. He never really talked about his past, either. I didn't even know if he had any brothers and sisters. I was about to ask him, but he gestured across from us, to the other side of the lawn.

"Shall we go and see what's so exciting over there?" he asked. He was pointing at a crowd across the park. I shrugged.

"Yeah, okay," I said. In my experience, people didn't tend to crowd up for good reasons, but we walked over holding hands and the delight of that outweighed any misgivings I might have had. There were people coming and going and if it had been something serious, I reckoned they would have looked more concerned. As it happened, everybody was relaxed and some people even smiled at us as we walked past, nodding a greeting.

As we neared the crowd, I spotted the source of the excitement – a van selling soft-serve. I felt myself grin. It was one of my most favorite things. I turned to see Brett looking at me, his eyes sparkling.

"Shall we get one?" he asked.

"Yes!" I said, giggling. "I haven't had one in years!"

We stopped at the van and Brett ordered our soft-serve. I felt a glimmer of excitement, looking at the high-piled creamy whiteness. I bit into it and shut my eyes – it tasted better than I remembered.

When I looked up, Brett was grinning. I frowned, though the corners of my lips were still lifted in a smile. He laughed.

"What?"

"I haven't seen anyone look so happy about anything in ages."

I laughed too. "It's one of my favorite things," I said, taking another lick. I saw him tense, and I realized that he was watching my pink tongue taking a lick of the dessert. I grinned, enjoying how it felt to have him look at me like that. He was staring with desire kindling in his eyes and I licked it again, deliberately exaggerating the gesture. He took a deep breath and I felt longing flare in my loins.

"So," he said, as we walked back past the bench, his voice tight but trying to sound casual. "You don't have any particular plans today? No important work to catch up or anything?"

"No," I said, feeling my skin tingle at the particular tone in his voice. He was still watching me eat and I could still see the flame of desire in his eyes. I made my voice light, though inside I was aching with longing. "Nothing important."

"Good," he replied. His voice was smoothed velvet. "So, after we've finished our soft-serve and walked around the park, we might go back to your apartment for a while?"

"Um, yes," I said. I swallowed hard, my throat tight with desire and longing. "We could, definitely."

"Good," he said again, and this time I could hear real satisfaction in his voice. We went back to the bench to eat our purchases.

We drove back to my apartment, and, even though my heart was racing with excitement, his hand warm where he stroked my thigh, I still found myself wondering about the mystery that surrounded him – sometimes he seemed a bit secretive, as though there was something that he was trying to hide, some story that was hidden from me. I hoped I would have a chance to discover more.

Chapter 15: Christina

I went for a long walk after Brett had gone home. I was dazed and amazed and mystified and delighted and I couldn't stop thinking about him. I went into the park – not the one where we'd walked, but a smaller one, close to my home – and sat down, letting my body relax as I watched the people walking here and there with their dogs or just by themselves, enjoying the warm evening.

"What is all this about?"

I shook my head. I should just stop thinking so hard and enjoy it. After all, he was being an absolute dear and I was finding out how fond I was of him. I just couldn't help questioning how he'd possibly gone from his difficult, arrogant former self, to this sweet person overnight.

"And why?"

He had been very awkward about his past, and I was starting to wonder exactly what was so interesting that he was worried people would sell it to the tabloids. It must be pretty intense, I imagined. I shook my head. I was letting my imagination get ahead of me. It was probably nothing. All the same, I imagined that perhaps he had been a spy, or he'd embezzled, or...well, a million possibilities. I went to the window, looking out.

"Get a grip, Christina," I told myself firmly. "You need something to distract you."

A distraction was easy to find – I had to prepare stuff for a meeting too and, even though I had decided to try and keep weekends free, I thought that it was better to focus on work than to try and make sense of all the events of today.

"Item one," I said aloud as I sat at my laptop. "I am falling for my boss. Item two, I don't know anything about him. Item three..." I paused, reaching for my notes from the meeting that I was actually supposed to be typing up. I put them down on the desk and resumed my own list. "Item three, he has some secrets and I don't know what they are."

I frowned. Was that really so bad? I didn't know why I was making such a big deal out of that – after all, there are loads of things you don't know about someone when you meet them for the first time. Everybody has hidden depths.

Hidden depths – like their past, their secrets, or where they might have stashed bodies...I tried not to think about it.

"That's just silly," I told myself.

After all, I was hiding things from him, too. I rested my face in my upturned palms and contemplated that fact. I hadn't told him anything about myself – nothing at all. He knew a little bit from that night when I'd been crying, and – as far as I knew – he hadn't even speculated about what had happened in my past. He'd certainly never asked me anything about it since then. I wondered about that – was he worried about upsetting me? Was it that he wasn't interested? Or, like me, was he too hesitant?

I sighed. I needed to do something – if I sat here and focused on work, or attempted to, I was going to go crazy. I reached for my coat and shrugged it on – it was starting to chill off a bit outside – and headed downstairs and out the door. As I was walking along the road, my phone rang.

I frowned. Normally, I'd ignore it. I would know if it was Neela, or Brett. And normally nobody else would phone me on a weekend, unless if it was someone from work. But it wasn't any of those possibilities. I took the call, thinking it was probably the plumber – I'd called him two days ago to ask about the cistern – it was leaking. I reckoned he was going to tell me when he could come and see to it.

"Hello?"

I felt my skin crawl as I recognized the voice on the other side. It wasn't the plumber. Or someone from work. Or even someone calling from the internet company. It was much worse than that.

It was my father.

"Christie! Hi. I'm calling from a hotel. I need help."

"What do you want?" My voice was hard as iron.

"Can't I just call my baby girl sometimes?" he wheedled. "Why would there need to be a reason?"

"Because you haven't called me in almost a decade?" I asked. I was deliberately trying to grow my anger – really, inside, I was terrified. I was resisting the urge to drop everything and run. Inside, my heart was pounding and my stomach was clenched and I couldn't breathe and I just wanted to roll up in a tiny ball.

"That can't be true," he said. "Well, I'm calling now."

I didn't know what to say, so I said what I thought. "How come?"

He took a breath. "I need help. I don't have any money and they're after me."

I stood there in the street. The cars went past, people went out for a stroll, children laughed and ran in the little park across the way. I didn't know what to say. I felt as if I was somehow in another place from those cheerful children, from the rush-hour traffic. I was not part of the comfortable, easy world. I was facing something I was terrified of.

"Fine," I said.

I hung up the phone and ran back to my apartment.

I didn't know what to do.

I sat down at my desk, numbly, and tried to think. I must be able to think of something.

Chapter 16: Brett

I drove home in a daze. I kept on thinking of Christina. All the way back to my apartment, thoughts of her floated through my head and I couldn't get her out of my mind. She was so sexy, so funny, so interesting. I kept on seeing her body – naked and beautiful – stretched out on the bed, her smile so gorgeous as she looked up at me with those big brown eyes. I kept on remembering what it felt like to hold her, to kiss her.

"Damn it, she's hot."

I blushed, despite the fact that there was nobody there to hear me. I had never felt like this before about anybody. Sure, I had a lot of experience, but I hadn't actually fallen in love before.

"Oh, heck."

I rested my hands on the dashboard as we stopped in heavy traffic. I hadn't really thought about it before, but that was what had happened. I'd had my eye on Christina for months and, now that I had really, well, met her...now I was developing feelings towards her that were more than just lustful.

I grinned, feeling a hardness in my loins just thinking about Christina.

This was weird for me – I'd always imagined that I'd never get attached to anyone, and now here I was, falling in love. I wasn't sure what to think about that. I would have imagined that I'd feel scared about that – after all, loving someone was a big deal, and generally speaking I wasn't that good with my emotions. If I thought about it, that was probably why I'd effectively pushed her away for months. But I wasn't anything but happy, I realized as the traffic cleared and I headed up towards my house. I

"I should have asked her about her past."

I couldn't forget that she had been crying that night – when we'd made love the first time after I found her at work. She had been very upset about something, and I'd never really made a deeper inquiry as to what it might have been. I guess I didn't want to remind her.

Whatever it was, just the memory of it terrified her.

The traffic was mercifully-swift – after all, it was Sunday afternoon – and I arrived back at my apartment in good time.

I leaned back on the couch. It was so strange that she had managed to hide any hint of the pain inside her for so long. When I first saw her, at work, I would have thought that her life was without any particular incident – she seemed so calm and self-contained. But, I thought with a grimace, you can never tell what's going on in someone else's life. You might think they're so serene and everything is perfect, but there's no way of really knowing until they tell you.

My mind wandered back to Christina, to her beautiful curves and how she gasped as I held her, my lips on her breast, my hand wandering over her soft, smooth waist and downwards, gripping her tight buttocks as I drew her against me, her legs parting for me to enter.

"Come on, Brett," I said to myself. I got up off the couch and went to my bedroom to get my forms from work. I was supposed to be finishing the budget meeting stuff. That was why I was here.

I found my mind wandering back to my conversation with Christina and how she always seemed to want to sidestep questions about her past. I dismissed the thoughts.

If I had wanted to find out about Christina, I should have stayed there with her. Speculating wasn't going to get answers.

I was just settling down to work when my phone rang. I swore inwardly.

"Hello?"

"Hi!" It was my brother. "How are you, Brett?"

"I'm fine," I said. My annoyance evaporated. "Good to hear you! How are things?" I felt relaxed, hearing his voice. There's something reassuring about a big brother, especially when you are navigating unknown territory, like I was. I wanted to ask him about Christina, but I couldn't just jump into it. I'd have to wait.

"Oh, fine," he said. He sounded genuinely positive, which was nice. "I had a great weekend – went out to go hiking...it's such great weather. You should join us sometime."

"Yeah," I said. "It was great weather." It was a warm day – I was tempted to open the window, but I left it for the moment. Even in this place, the traffic could get pretty loud. "Did you go anywhere particular?" Maybe he had some good ideas about where to go for a hike and I could take Christina there sometime.

"Not really. I always go to the same hill. It's a nice walk, and I'm challenging myself – I want to do it in an hour and a half."

I shook my head. "Damn it! You can't stop being a pro, can you?" I tensed, the moment I'd said it.

"That's not amusing, considering."

I swallowed hard. I hadn't meant it like that. I knew that since the accident, he'd regretted the end of his career, but I hadn't meant to be referencing that. I knew he would take it like that, though. I meant that despite it, he still...I sighed. I guess it was a bit callous.

"Sorry," I said quickly. "It was a stupid thing to say."

"Quite." my brother said. It was a weird expression for him to use, but I ignored it and tried to think of something else to say.

"Um...so, is it a good hike? For beginners, I mean?" I asked. "I mean, if I were to take someone there who had no clue what they were doing, would they manage it safely?"

"Sure," my brother said. He sounded more like himself, and I was glad of that. I hadn't meant to say something stupid that referenced his accident. I hadn't really, but I could understand that it meant that to him. He had literally gone from professional to unable to play and I knew how much it had hurt him and how long it took for him to come to terms with it and start a new life. "It's quite easy – there aren't any bits that need climbing. You could manage it in a few hours, I think. It's well-suited to beginners."

"Thanks," I said. I laughed. "That makes me feel like you have a lot of faith in my training."

He was laughing too, now. "You know what I mean," he said, chuckling. "It takes me two and a half hours now. I don't think it'll take you much longer, and even a complete beginner would get it done in four. It's a nice walk."

"Thanks," I said. "And if I brought someone reasonably fit along, they'd be fine too."

He sighed. "Yes. As I said, anyone could manage it. Are you seeing someone?" he asked directly. I stared at the phone, astonished by how quickly he'd assessed my motives.

"Why would you conclude that?" I asked, though I was laughing now too. He really was way ahead.

"Well," my brother said. "I never heard you want to get out into the outdoors before. Not in such a big way."

"I do like the outdoors," I said, laughing as I spoke.

"Well, yes, I guess. But you have never asked me about a hike before."

"No," I agreed. "I guess that I haven't, no." I shook my head. "Damn it...you are a natural big brother, aren't you?"

He laughed. "I try to be," he agreed. "Well, are you going to tell me more details?"

"About what?" I felt guarded. How I felt about Christina was so new and so beautiful to me and, though I really wanted to get my brother's advice on this, I also felt the need to keep some of that information to myself.

"About the new girl, Brett," he said lightly. "Who is she? Can I at least know where she's from?"

I sighed. "Sure. She's a girl I met at work. She works for me. I guess that should be a problem, hey?" I tensed. I personally didn't see it as wrong, but I was sure not everybody would share my views on that. I waited for my brother to judge me – he was always a bit judgmental and I had come to expect it.

"Um...well, I don't know," he said. I tensed. I'd been waiting for the judgment, and there it was.

"Yeah, I know...it's not appropriate, and all that stuff," I began tensely. "But..."

"It's not about that," my brother interrupted quickly. "It's about how does she feel, Brett? You know how it is – she might feel pressure, since you own the company..."

"Thanks!" I said, outraged. "Thanks a lot, man. You mean to say that she's only interested in me because I'm her boss? That she feels coerced and pressured and that's the only reason someone'd look sideways at me?" My reaction was sudden, but I guessed he'd stepped on raw nerves.

"I didn't say that, Brett," my brother replied. He sounded quite calm. "I never suggested that she wouldn't look at you if..."

"Yeah, but you did say that the only reason she's looking at me is because she's scared that if she turns me down, she'll be unemployed. Damn it!" I was hurt. I was also scared. It was just possible that he was right.

Christina had acted like she hated me until just recently. Had I inadvertently pressured her that night, forcing her to change her attitude? I gasped, just thinking of it.

"Brett, calm down," my brother said patiently. Telling someone to calm down – which is, in fact, a command – doesn't have the effect of making someone feel calmer. It makes them feel threatened or judged, and I felt both.

"Calm down! No, I damn well can't be calm." I was furious now. "I'm insulted, and I don't think I'm going to continue this conversation. Maybe we should talk tomorrow." I took a deep breath, struggling to get a hold on feelings that even I knew were unreasonable.

"Maybe," my brother agreed. "I'll phone soon." He sounded relaxed, but I couldn't be sure.

I stood up, to find I was shaking. I went through to the kitchen and made some coffee and something to eat – being tired and hungry isn't known for its benefits to decision-making – and when I had eaten and drunk, I tried to think logically about what my brother said.

"He didn't say that she was feeling coerced. He said she might be."

I had to admit, that could be correct. I hadn't actually even thought that she might be, but it was something I should ask about. I would take an opportunity to ask her about it tomorrow, I decided. She should be able to tell me, if that was true, and it was something that I certainly wanted to know.

I would ask her tomorrow after work. I just had to think of a way of raising the subject properly.

Chapter 17: Christina

I looked out over the apartment-blocks, the lights bright against the blackness beyond my windows, the traffic blaring down below and the car headlights shining against the inky dark. I shivered, wrapping my cardigan tight around me, though it was not particularly cold. I could still hear my father's voice and I didn't know what to do to calm down.

"I should tell Neela."

I sat down heavily on the couch, resting my head in my hands. I couldn't tell Neela! I had never told her the particulars about my situation – even though I trusted her, I didn't trust anyone she might accidentally tell. People can be so cruel, and knowing that I didn't have the same background as them might cause me big trouble at work.

I needed to tell somebody, though. I had to get some advice from somewhere.

I wished I could tell Brett.

"No. Absolutely not."

I didn't know him that well. What would he think? He would be shocked, that I was sure of. He wouldn't want to be associated with someone who was from such a different walk of life to himself. I was sure that he would disapprove. I didn't know him well enough to turn to him for help.

I went through to my bedroom, stifling a yawn. It was late. I should go to bed.

I sat down heavily on the bed, drained of energy. I had stuff to prepare for tomorrow, but I couldn't focus. My head was swimming and I felt so tired, yet at the same time my heart was thudding and I was wide awake.

My phone rang as I reached for the report I was checking through. I froze.

Should I answer it?

I had no idea. I flipped open the case and felt my heart sink. It was an unknown number. What were the chances that it was my father, calling again from anther phone?

I took a deep breath and answered it.

"Hello," the voice that I had been expecting, yet fearing, replied. "Christie. It's me. Is your apartment in Brookford House?"

"What?"

I dropped the phone on the bed. It was my father! And, yes...My apartment is in Brookford House. But how the hell did he know that? And why did he want to know?

"Why do you want to know?" I demanded angrily. I had wanted to sound intimidating, but really all I sounded was frightened.

"Because I'm in the park. I'm trying to find you. Christie...won't you talk to me?" His tone was wheedling, like it had been when he noticed that he'd scared me.

"No," I said.

I slammed the phone shut, put it down on the bed and rolled into a ball. This man had terrorized my childhood – swearing, screaming abuse, threatening – and I had been grateful to escape him. Uncle Hal had paid for my education and I owed him, more than anyone else, the fact that I had become who I'd become. School had been an escape from my terrible home. It had also been an escape from my father. There was no way I was going to let him into the life I'd built for myself. No way at all.

"He said he was in the park. He knows where I live."

I tried to think of how he could have gotten that information, and then I remembered that my CV was up on my LinkedIn profile and it happened to have my postal address on it, which is the same as my living address. How hard would it have been for him to find it?

"Damn it!" I swore.

I was frightened. If I knew anything about him at all, he was here because he needed something. And if he needed something, he wasn't going to just stay outside in the park, or at a hotel or wherever. He was going to come and find me.

I felt a wash of fear go through me. I knew it was irrational to feel like this – after all, here I was high up in the building, with a security door on the outside – but I couldn't help it. I didn't want to end up cowering in my apartment all night, waiting for the knock on the door, the shouts outside, the yells and threats like when I was a child. I was going somewhere.

I grabbed my suitcase and threw a handful of clothes in at random, lifted my high-heels off the floor and threw them in too. I packed my brush, makeup, toothbrush, a belt, my slippers. After grabbing one or two more items, I shut the case, reached for my car-keys, shrugged on my coat and, my handbag in my hand, marched down to the lift.

I held my breath as we went down – every second, I was expecting him to get into the lift, or to hear the door open and have him shout my name. But we went down to the ground floor without incident, and I got out and went to find my car, hands shaking.

"Please, let me get away quickly."

I threw my suitcase and handbag into the car, jumped into the driver's seat, slammed the door, and turned the key in the ignition. I shot off towards the doors.

I was planning as I drove. I would go to Neela's. Maybe I could think of some way of explaining to her why I was there, something that didn't involve my father or anything else. I could tell her I was stressed, maybe. That she would understand. I hoped she wouldn't mind if I stayed there. I wouldn't be there for long...just a few days. Just long enough to be sure that my father was going to leave me alone.

I drove across town, amazed by how busy the city was. It was Sunday night, at about nine, and cars and people were everywhere, the neon lights harsh from the shops and bars and clubs, the traffic loud. I leaned on my steering-wheel as we halted at the lights, trying not to breathe so fast.

"Calm, Christina. Breathe in, and out. In, and out."

I put my foot on the clutch and jolted forward, then sped off as I started up again. I was almost at Neela's apartment building.

I found a parking-space eventually, stopped the car, grabbed my stuff and went to ring the doorbell.

"Hello?" Neela's voice sounded sleepy. I was so grateful she'd not just ignored a ring at the doorbell on a Sunday night.

"Neela! It's me!" I said urgently. "Christina Bradfield."

"Christina?"

"Yes," I said, hearing the utter disbelief in her voice. I never called without some kind of arrangement. It just didn't happen. "Let me in?"

"Sure, Christina!" Neela said, her voice light. "Just have to tidy away a few things..." she pressed the bell, and I pushed the door open. By the time I got into the lobby, I was shaking. Out on the street, I'd been scared my father could somehow venture over on this side of town and find me. I went to the lift and went up, still shivering.

"Christina!" Neela greeted as I arrived outside her door. "Hey! Come in...hell, you look so pale!"

"Please, just let me in," I said, then went hurriedly into her apartment while she locked the door behind us and then turned to face me, frowning.

"Christina?" she asked gently. "What the heck happened? Why are you so scared?"

I let out a deep breath. "Sorry, Neela," I said. "I just...well...Sorry. Can I have a moment? I need to go to the bathroom and shower and try and calm down."

"Sure, Christina," she said, looking at me oddly. "Hell...are you sure I can't get something for you? You really look like you're in shock or something."

I shook my head. I was fine. I just needed to be somewhere safe.

"No. Thanks, Neela. I'm just going to go and get that shower now."

"Sure," Neela agreed. Her big dark eyes looked after me worriedly. I went into the bathroom and locked it behind me. I felt safe now. I stood there for a long moment, just trying to get my bearings. I had stopped shaking, and anger was starting to replace the rank fear. I shouldn't be chased out of my own home by somebody! I had a right to feel safe in my own home. I unbuttoned my blouse and undressed, getting into the shower.

I had stayed at Neela's once or twice, and I grinned to myself at the floral shower-gel decorated with pictures of bubbles, the shower-head that had been mended where it had fallen and cracked, cracking one of the tiles with it. I didn't think that anyone, looking at Neela, would guess at how quirky she was.

I was much calmer after a warm shower. I dried off and dressed and went to join Neela in the sitting-room.

"Hey. Feeling better?" she asked. She was sitting on the couch, a mug of something in between her hands. She gestured to me. "Yours is on the table."

"Thanks," I said. I took the cup and sipped, feeling revived as I tasted the warm, sweet taste. I shut my eyes, letting myself calm down. After a shower, and with cocoa to drink, I felt much safer.

"You don't have to tell me what happened, if you don't want." Neela watched me across the table, dark eyes solemn.

I shrugged. "Thanks, Neela," I said. I felt uncomfortable. I wanted to tell her something – after all, I couldn't very well turn up and ask to be put up for the night without giving some kind of an explanation – and yet, it wasn't easy.

She spoke as I cleared my throat. "You could sleep in the bed, but I'd probably wake you up – I move a lot."

I laughed. "Thanks, Neela. You're an absolute angel. I'll sleep on the couch. If I really can't sleep, I might have to take you up on your offer, though." I laughed shakily. "I am pretty stressed out."

"Yeah," she said. "I wish I could do something to help. Have you had dinner?"

"No," I said. I had actually forgotten about dinner. It wasn't a bad idea. My stomach rumbled at the thought. "Can I cook something?"

"Yeah," she nodded. "That would be great. I haven't eaten much either – I wasn't hungry. I am now, though. So, let's make something!"

I grinned and nodded. Somehow she had managed to make this all feel like we were on a holiday, not like I'd just driven here in the middle of the night to get away from my flat. It felt a bit surreal, going and cooking with Neela. I was still stressed, my body racing with adrenalin, though I'd stopped shaking and I felt a bit calmer. We went through to the dining-area where she had a big table, just on the other side of the kitchen counter.

"I had to come here," I said as we ate. She didn't say anything, just waited to let me talk. I swallowed awkwardly. "I got a phone-call from someone from my past. He had my address. I was scared he'd find me."

"I see," Neela nodded. She looked worried; her brow crinkled with a frown. "Christina, couldn't you maybe get hold of the police about this?"

"No," I said. I was touched that she was so concerned, but I knew that wasn't a route available to me right now. "I can't really report someone for calling me – that's not a crime."

"If he threatened you, I think it must count for something," Neela said.

I shrugged. "I don't know."

We both ate in silence for a while. I felt better as I ate, the food imparting energy to me. I started to feel my brain coming out of the shock and I took a sip of water, wondering about what to tell Neela. She was eating calmly and she hadn't seemed inclined to ask me any more questions. I thought it was best to leave it like it was for now.

"We can go into work together tomorrow," she said.

"Thanks!" I grinned. Fortunately, I'd brought my work things with me, along with a change of clothes. "I'd appreciate that." I wanted to avoid my apartment for as long as possible. I knew him – hanging around until I came out for my commute to work – or back from work – would be just the sort of thing he would do. I wondered, fleetingly, where he was staying the night. I was sure he must have somewhere – after all, if he got all the way to New York, he must have means of some sort. Why he would choose to spend them on finding me, I had no idea.

"No problem," Neela agreed. "And then maybe after work, I can go back to your apartment with you? How likely is this crazy guy to stop bothering you?"

I shrugged again. "I don't know." I couldn't imagine how long it would take him to give up – after all, if he'd come all this way, I couldn't expect him to just leave after one night.

"Are you sure we shouldn't tell the police?" Neela asked. "I mean...just in case they can do something?"

"I don't know – I guess I don't want to get the law involved just yet. Not unless we know it's serious."

She leaned back and regarded me across the table, dark eyes wide and full of care. "I understand," she said gently. "But if something even slightly weird happens – if you get a call and he threatens you again, or anything – I really think we ought to do something. At least, we could tell Durrell – he could beat the guy up!"

I laughed. Durrell was her boyfriend. I hadn't thought that they were that seriously involved, but clearly I had missed something. She had that happy look in her eye simply from hearing his name. I knew how that felt, because I felt the same thing for somebody else now.

I wondered again if I should tell Brett. I just couldn't let him know what it was that I was so scared of. I finished my dinner and went to do the washing up. Neela finished up and came in after me.

"I'll go and get some things from the cupboard," she said, drying plates and putting them away carefully. "You need a duvet and pillow."

"Thanks," I said, grinning at her as she reached for the drying-up cloth. "You're being so wonderful...I hope you know that."

She just smiled. "You're my friend, Christina. Friends help each other."

"Thanks," I said again and gave her a big hug. She hugged me back and I felt tears spring to my eyes. It was so wonderful to have someone like a sister. I blinked, feeling tears running down my cheeks. If I was wearing any makeup, it would be smudged terribly by now.

"Now, I'll go get those things," Neela said. She was emotional too – I could hear it in how her voice wobbled a bit as she talked. I knew she was trying to hide it, and I bent over the sink, finishing with the dishes.

I went to bed on the couch about half an hour later. It was still early, but I was exhausted and drained.

I pulled the coverlet up over my shoulders and rested my head on the big fluffy pillow. She'd put down a sheet for me and blankets, in case I was cold in the night. I felt a twist in my heart, seeing how kind she'd been to me. I hadn't looked at my phone since the last call – it was in my handbag that rested next to the couch. I didn't want to know if he'd tried to call again. I didn't want to think about it until tomorrow morning.

I shut my eyes, feeling surprisingly sleepy. I wondered what I would do if I saw Brett tomorrow, and whether I would find the courage to tell him where I was.

Chapter 18: Brett

I drove into work early the next morning. It had been a long, restless night. I couldn't get the thought out of my mind that Christina might just be sleeping with me because she couldn't say no to her boss. I didn't want to believe that.

"I am going to ask her."

I parked smartly in the ground-floor parking, sprinted to the elevator and got in. I got out at the third floor where the finance offices were and where my office was at the front of the hallway with the big window looking out over the busy traffic.

"Christina?" I murmured. I was outside her office, but the door was closed. I knocked, but nobody was there. I wondered if I should try the door. Maybe she hadn't heard me? It was unusual for her to be late. I went back to my office.

I didn't want to disturb her if she was on an important call.

I sat down at my desk, feeling my spirits lift. The investors had received our presentation extremely well, and it looked like the capital we needed for the expansion was coming in. I allowed myself a moment of excitement. This would allow our company to grow to almost double its size in the next decade. I wasn't just excited about the profits – though of course that was exciting too – but about employing people.

We were creating hundreds of new jobs.

I let myself feel excited about that, forgetting the disappointment of not being able to talk to Christina. Maybe it was better that I got my words sorted.

I still didn't know exactly how to address it with her.

I worked until ten o' clock, mostly writing emails, and then I went out to get coffee. I couldn't resist checking Christina's office again as I went past the printing-room.

I felt bad. I was starting to wonder if my brother hadn't been right. If she didn't even feel close enough to me to let me know something like that, maybe I had coerced her.

"Stop stressing so much," I told myself – after all, it was just what my brother had said, getting to me.

"Brett?" my CTO asked, coming up behind me as I walked into my office. I'd forgotten I'd asked him here to meet and discuss the new equipment. I nodded to him, trying to look unconcerned and confident.

"Hi. Sorry. I was distracted. Come in. How was your weekend?"

"Fine, thanks." He grinned. "I went hiking, actually. It was such great weather, I had to go outside."

"Great." I reached for the papers that had the information I needed to discuss. I felt restless – I didn't really want to be sitting, talking about the latest in printing technology so tediously: I wanted to sitting in Christina's office, talking about stuff that really mattered.

I eventually settled and had a productive discussion. I was pleased when the questions were cleared up.

"Thanks, Brett. See you at lunch."

"Yeah. I might work through lunch," I replied. He looked surprised. I bent over my desk, looking over an email from one of our board members. I really didn't intend to work through lunch – my intention was to go and find Christina and spend the lunch hour chatting with her. I really wanted to get my concerns out of the way. I tried to focus on jotting down notes from the discussion I'd just had, but I couldn't focus and after a while I gave up and stood. It wouldn't do any harm to check if she was there and ask her for lunch, I thought swiftly.

I walked past her office again, to find the door open. A young woman was there, a frown on her brow.

"What's up?" I asked, coming and leaning in the doorway. "Is Ms. Bradfield needed for something?"

"Morning, Mr. Caden," the young woman greeted me. I recognized her as the secretary for the finance department. "Yes. I needed Christina to sign this form. I'll just leave it for her – she can do it tomorrow."

"Is Christina in?" I asked, frowning. "I mean, did she come in?" It looked like she hadn't been here all morning.

"She called in sick," the woman said.

"Oh." I felt my frown deepen.

"Did you have to give her a message?" the secretary asked me.

"Um, no," I replied, wondering if I should call Christina to ask what happened. "No worries. It can wait."

"Have a nice day, Mr. Caden."

"Thanks." I smiled and did my best to look friendly, but inside my heart was racing. I went swiftly back to my office and shut the door. I didn't want anybody to disturb me if I was going to call Christina.

"That is paranoid," I told myself. "She was fine last week."

She had been in to work every day after that night when we'd first made love together. If she had objected so strongly, wouldn't she have said something then?

But not if she felt too intimidated, I reminded myself. Not if she was too scared to say no to me.

The thought made me feel horrible. I couldn't bear it. If I'd forced myself on Christina I wouldn't be able to sleep at night. It didn't matter that she hadn't apparently objected – it mattered that she wanted to.

"You're being silly."

I tried to get a hold on this. I had no evidence that she had stayed off work to avoid me – that was pure imagination on my part. I had no evidence to speak of that she had hated being with me. All I had that made me think that was my brother's words, stuck in my head, and I couldn't get them out no matter how I pushed them down.

I pulled out my phone, to check that she hadn't messaged me. She hadn't. There was nothing to stop me getting hold of her. I paused –

should I call or should I text? I felt that she might not want to talk to me.

I knew it was just my imagination that she was avoiding me – she might really be sick. At the same time, I hesitated to call her on my phone – if she refused to answer it, that was a good indication that she really was mad at me. Even though it would make things a bit clearer, I didn't actually want to find out.

I decided to call her from the landline. If she picked up, good. If she didn't, I'd just have to wait until tomorrow. Or try and get hold of her another way.

I sighed, put my mobile back in my pocket and called her number on my office phone.

No reply.

I leaned back in my chair and put the phone down, feeling confused and upset, even though I knew I had no reason to be. It was understandable, really – after all, most people don't pick up the phone to numbers they don't know. In itself, that meant nothing. I went ahead and texted her anyway, even though I had this weird feeling that she might not want to hear from me.

Hey Christina. I saw you weren't at work. I hope you're okay.

I sent it. I reckoned that couldn't do any harm. After all, even a colleague would be permitted to write something so neutral, especially if they discovered she was off sick.

I felt better after having sent a message. I turned to my computer and tried to concentrate on the emails I had to reply to, but my mind was focused down the hallway in Christina's empty office and I couldn't stop thinking about her.

Chapter 19: Christina

I was standing in a shop in the mall when my phone went. I was dressed for work – nice white silky blouse, black slacks, high heels – and people were looking at me strangely. I wanted to say that I meant to go to work this morning. The small problem was that, when I got there, someone was waiting for me.

I still felt sick.

I had walked up the stairs after parking my car, and there he was. Bold as brass, not even bothering to get out of the way of people who were hurrying past him into the big front doors. He was wearing a stained hoodie and trousers and he'd looked exactly like he had when I was young – angry, entitled and needy, all at once. I'd panicked and run.

My feet gave out after a hundred meters down the sidewalk, and I'd run into the mall – crowded spaces are the safest spaces. It was something I'd learned early on. Disappearing into a crowd could save your life. I'd spent the last three hours wandering around the mall, trying to figure out a strategy to get my car back and get home. I'd called in sick at work – I wasn't going back there today. I remembered that my phone had buzzed and I wondered if it was Neela, looking for me.

I pulled my phone out. It was a message from Brett. I stepped out of the way of a lady with an armful of clothing and went around the corner to read it.

Hey Christina. I saw you weren't at work. I hope you're okay.

I let out a sigh. He had noticed I wasn't there, and I felt bad because I was skipping work for no good reason. He sounded worried – I knew him well enough by now to know that he didn't tend to express emotions like worry or fear. The very terseness of it suggested to me that he was upset. I hastily wrote a reply.

Sorry, Brett...I couldn't come in today. I'm fine.

I sent the message and then as the sales assistant came over, I pretended to be absorbed in feeling the quality of a suede blazer.

"We have them in all sizes." She was a young woman wearing a black uniform with thick makeup and an earnest smile.

"Thanks," I said.

I pretended to contemplate the blazers a bit longer, just until she had gone over to the front of the store. Then I walked out and went to find another place to think. My feet took me to a café. I ordered a coffee and sat down to contemplate what I could do.

I had two options. Either I could hide out here until lunchtime, when I could call Neela and ask her to help. Or I could risk going back to work to get my car, and driving to my apartment.

The first option felt a lot nicer, except that I had work I desperately needed to do. I could stay here in the café for another three hours and work, ordering coffee on a regular basis until lunchtime, I guessed – but it would be good to go home. I just didn't know if I could face seeing my father again.

"Someone would have moved him on," I told myself firmly. There was no way security was going to let anyone hang around outside the doors for hours without at least asking them what they were doing there. I had to at least check if he was still there.

I took a deep breath, called the waiter over and paid for my coffee. I would walk over to my office and check out what was going on.

As I went to the ground floor, my phone rang. It was Neela.

"Hi!" I greeted breathlessly. "How's everything?"

"I just went past your office to chat. I noticed you weren't there. Is something up?" She sounded concerned.

I swallowed hard. "I'm fine. Actually, I'm at the mall – near where we go to have lunch. Maybe you could come and chat at lunchtime?" I checked the time on the clock across the room – it was eleven a.m. I could work here for another hour before going across to our usual café for lunch.

"Um, sure, Christina," Neela agreed. "I'll be over there at half past twelve."

"Great," I replied.

I wondered, afterwards, why I'd done that.

I guess everybody should know when they can't take on something alone – that's a mature thing to be able to do, to ask for help. I couldn't take this on alone and it was time I acknowledged that. It was time I told somebody what was going on in my life.

I worked on the budget for an hour and then paid for the two coffees I'd ordered during that time, packing my things away and going to the café across the street. I went to our table at the back and, after half an hour – during which I worked and ordered water – Neela came in.

"Hey!" she greeted me, a big smile on her face. She was wearing bright red lipstick and a gorgeous black-and-white pants suit that looked stunning on her angular form. She sat down opposite me. "Great to see you. I guess I should order something."

"I haven't ordered lunch either," I said with a smile. "So good to see you, Neela. I guess I have a lot of explaining to do," I added, feeling bad.

"Not at all," Neela said. "Hell, Christina! I'm your friend. You don't owe me anything."

I felt an ache in my heart. Nobody had ever told me that – nobody besides Brett, weirdly, had ever made me feel that comfortable, as if I was enough in myself. I took a deep breath, smiling at her. "Thanks," I said.

We ordered our usual sandwiches, and I tried to think of what to say, how to tell her my story. At the end of a few minutes, I launched straight in.

"I came from a pretty rough background," I began. "I grew up on the wrong side of town, in the best apartment my father could afford by then, which wasn't great. He was...well, he was addicted to gambling. Probably still is. He kept on thinking he'd hit a big win and make all the money back." I sniffed, remembering how angry that used to make me, the emotion still raw and burning inside. "I remember how he used to come back late at night, roaring drunk, shouting and talking loudly with his friends. And how if I did anything – if I sneezed, for pity's sake – there could be hell on earth. He'd lose it completely, shouting and swearing at me."

My friend just looked at me, eyes full of tenderness.

"I finally got away from there when I was fifteen. My uncle Hal paid for me to go to high school in another town. I boarded there and only saw my father sometimes after that. Throughout college the one thing I dreaded – worse than exams, worse than anything – was when he would come and visit. It always happened unexpectedly. He'd turn up and usually try to get stuff out of me – money, information. I had almost no allowance – I relied on my housemates to feed me. I worked for years to pay off my college debt, and I never got a chance to pay back my uncle."

I was sobbing now, tears running down my cheeks. I was aware that we were surrounded by people, but I couldn't hold back. I sniffed, dabbing my face with a paper napkin. Neela reached out and took my hand.

"I'm so sorry, Christina," she said softly. "I'm so sorry that happened to you."

I sniffed again, taking a deep breath. "You didn't do anything," I said, smiling at her and drying off my tears. "You don't have anything to be sorry for."

She smiled. "I do – I am sorry that I wasn't available for you to tell me before, that I didn't act like someone you could trust."

I shook my head. "Neela, that isn't your fault. I learned not to trust. It's not your fault that it didn't occur to me to trust you."

She nodded, but I could see how emotional she felt. "I guess," she said carefully. "Anyhow. I'm so glad you told me now. Shall we order dessert?"

I chuckled. "That sounds like a great plan. I could do with something more to eat."

We finished our lunch in companionable quiet.

"My father is the person who's stalking me," I said as we finished our coffees. "That's why I'm so frightened and why I can't say anything. No matter how vile he was, I don't want him going to jail."

Neela looked at me compassionately. "Christina, I understand," she said gently. "If there's anything I can do – like maybe talking to him on the phone next time he calls – just tell me."

I nodded slowly. "That's really kind of you, Neela," I said gently. "But I couldn't possibly lay that on you."

She just smiled kindly and I knew that she would do her best to help me. I just couldn't expose her to his lying manipulations. I would feel like I was putting myself at his mercy, letting him contact my only friends.

We finished lunch and I paid the bill – it was the least I could do. Neela gave me a hug as we went out through the door into the street. I held tightly onto her, the caring gesture bringing tears to my eyes again. I was feeling so emotional! I squeezed her hard and looked up at her, blinking back tears.

"I'll walk back with you," I said. "I might as well get my car."

Neela nodded, grinning at me. "Good idea. And if we see that guy, we'll sort him out."

I grinned back. I couldn't imagine what we – as two slim, smartly-dressed businesswomen – were going to do about it, but then again I was sure that the pair of us could take on almost anything together.

It felt good having someone to get my back.

We walked up to the building and I let out a sigh of relief. He'd gone! I felt weak with the sudden drop in my tension levels. I looked up at Neela, who had stopped on the sidewalk to wait with me while I took stock of the front step.

"He's gone," I said. Even I could hear the sound of deep relief in my voice. "I'll get the car and drive back to my apartment. I think I can spend the night there by myself tonight." I sounded confident.

"Are you sure?" Neela asked, concerned.

"I'm sure I'll be fine," I said. I was amazed by how strong I felt. "If he tries anything funny, I really will call the cops. He would have asked for it if he actually threatens me."

"That's quite right," Neela agreed. "You have no need to be scared."

"Thanks."

I gave her a quick hug, then waved as I hurried around to the car-park. She went off up the stairs and I stepped quickly around the side of the building towards where I'd parked. I looked about quickly – there was nobody here waiting for me. I found my car, still where I'd left it this morning, and unlocked it, then drove swiftly out the gate and towards my apartment.

I was amazed by how much lighter I felt, since I'd confided my story to somebody. She had received it so kindly, with no judgment and no speculation – she'd just let me talk until my heart was freer. I slowed down at the stoplight and waited, and I was surprised by how excited I felt about getting back to my own home. It would be so good to sleep in a bed, and be able to cook my own dinner! Not that I hadn't loved staying with Neela – it would just feel good to be independent.

I drove around the corner, and my mind wandered to Brett. I couldn't decide what I should tell him. I reckoned it was best to leave him thinking I was sick – we didn't know each other so well yet and I couldn't guess how he would receive my story. I would feel better if I could wait a while and get to know him better before I shared the story of my past with him.

I drove up to my apartment block and around the back. I would be pleased to sleep for a bit before I got down to the last bit of work I had to do for the day.

Chapter 20: Brett

I worked late that evening. I don't know why – I guess some small part of me still waited to receive word from Christina. Or maybe I hoped she would come into work at some point during the day.

"Mr. Caden? Is it okay if I go home now?" My secretary asked from the doorway. I looked up, nodding at her over the top of my laptop.

"Sure," I said. "What time is it?"

"It's six-thirty, Mr. Caden."

"Oh. Great. Thanks, Terri."

"No problem, Mr. Caden."

I bent back to my work, the sound of her high-heeled shoes clicking on the floor as she walked down the stairs across from my office. I turned my attention back to the screen, where I was just adding the finishing touches to a yearly report for the board. It wasn't due yet for another month, but I wanted to check through what had been written and get it done and off the list.

I read through the copy again, yawning. I was hungry and a bit tired. It was probably time to go home, I thought, blinking under the bright lights of the office. I reached for my phone.

I had a reply from Christina!

I felt my heart thump as I saw it, but was surprised by the brevity. It just said that she was fine. It could have been written for anybody, not for somebody she was particularly fond of.

"Brett, you're overreacting now."

I put the phone back in my pocket. I was being silly. She had replied, and that mattered to me, a great deal. It had been sent just before midday, I noticed. At least I knew that she was okay. I had no idea if she was really fine, or if she just meant she was a bit sick, but I decided to assume that she really had taken off work because she felt ill. She'd never done it before, so I knew that she wasn't just taking off because she wanted to. It was for some serious reason or other.

"Like, maybe, because she wants to avoid me."

I laughed at my insecurities. Of course, that wasn't it. Why would she bother replying if she was mad at me?

I went out and took the lift down to the ground floor, heading down to get my car.

On the way back, my phone rang. The traffic had already thinned out a great deal. I was at a stoplight and I pulled it out.

It was my brother, Teagan.

"Hey, Brett?"

"Hey, Teagan," I replied, feeling reassured by hearing his voice. "How are you? Can't talk...I'm in traffic – I just need to put it on speaker..."

I sat it on the dashboard, ready to talk.

"I just wanted to ask if you want to come over for dinner tonight," my brother asked. "I know it's short notice, but if you don't have any other plans, I will get it going and have it cooked by around seven pm?"

"Oh!" I felt my stomach growling. It would be great to have a dinner ready-made, and I would welcome some company. It sure beat spending time by myself at home worrying about Christina. "Great."

"That's great," my brother replied, sounding pleased. "I'll go and stick the dinner in the oven, so it's ready when you get in."

"Thanks!" I was genuinely pleased. "I'm on my way."

I put my foot on the gas after slipping my phone back into my pocket, hurrying up the street.

I got there with ten minutes to spare.

My brother lived on the top floor. I got out and rang the bell and was pleased when he answered it, his cheerful voice drifting down to me where I waited on the top step in the cool air.

"Hey, Teagan," I greeted. "It's me."

"Great! I'll let you in now." He sounded enthusiastic to hear me, which made me feel happy too.

"Hey! Brett, come in!" my brother greeted me as I took the lift to the top floor. It was only three floors, the building where he lived, but I took the lift anyway. He was waiting at the door to let me in.

"Hey, great to see you," I said, pausing to shake his hand and being swamped in an embrace. My brother is a good few inches taller than me, which makes him very tall indeed, and he has big shoulders and arms still from all those hours in training with a baseball bat. He stepped back, looking at me, squarish face lit with a smile.

"So good that you could be here, Brett. Come in! Come in." He stepped back, letting me pass through into the hallway, where a delicious smell floated up from the kitchen.

"Man, that smells amazing," I commented, following him to the kitchen.

"Good! It's a vegetable curry. I baked bread to go with it, too – all totally free of animal products."

"Wow," I said, genuinely impressed. My brother had become vegan recently, and I was full of admiration for the time and effort it involved. I also had to admit that the few times I'd eaten his cooking, it was super-good. This vegan thing had something to recommend it, I thought with a grin as I sat down at the kitchen table.

"Thanks, man," he said, noticing that I had brought some wine along with me. "That'll be great. And it's a Cabernet Sauvignon, too – well chosen." He went to fetch the salad and put it on the table, which was already set with some really nice gray-black plates and cutlery.

"So, how was your day?" I asked, as I helped him carry things over to the table.

"It was a good day," my brother said, taking the plate over to the table. I went to join him. "I didn't have a lot of work today...had a chat with some guys from the development baseball group. They're doing great things for kids from disadvantaged homes." He grinned. "One of our guys is looking to play semi-professionally already."

"That's so great," I said. He looked so happy for those kids. "You know, Teagan, I'm so proud of you."

"What?" Teagan said. He had tears in his eyes, his face a picture of pure shock, and I felt my heart ache as he blinked them away. "What?" he asked again, sounding uncertain. "You serious?"

I nodded, feeling terrible that I'd never realized how important it was to say that to him. "Of course! Hell, you're my big brother, Teagan the baseball star,"

"Brett," he said, after a long moment during which he tried to get a hold on himself. "You know how much that means to me. You see, I always felt that you were so mega-successful. Mom was so proud of you, and when I got my injury and I couldn't play, I felt like I'd let everyone down."

I felt tears in my own eyes. "Teagan!" I said, shaking my head fondly. "How could you say that? Mom adored you. Frankly, I got the impression that you were her favorite son."

"No way!" he laughed aloud, disbelief on his face. He passed me the plate of bread and I took some, already eating my stew. I raised a brow. "You didn't know?"

"No!" he was laughing again, shaking his head in confusion. "You mean, you thought that Mom preferred me, out of us brothers?"

"Of course," I said, fairly sure that was obvious.

He shook his head. "Brad, you know...you'll have to believe me when I say that I never saw it like that. I always saw it the other way."

It was my turn to stare at him. "You really thought that Mom put more effort into looking after me?"

He shrugged. "More time. So, yeah, I guess, more effort. I don't know why I felt like that. I just felt as if you mattered more, like you got everything right. I can't believe I've never talked about this before."

I nodded. "I know. It's taken thirty years for us to finally address this. And the more I think about it, the more I realize that the way she treated us was actually fair."

"Yeah," my brother said. "It was equitable, not equal."

I stared at him. "You're right," I said. Strangely, just knowing that made years of misunderstanding suddenly wash off me, my heart healing in places where it was sore before.

"Yeah!" Teagan grinned. "It's only now that I get to thinking about it that it becomes so clear." He reached for another helping of curry, taking a slice of bread to eat with it. somehow it seemed as if we'd become closer, as if a barrier that I'd never even known was there had gone, letting us talk with real trust.

I could see that he was close to tears, and I felt that way too. I hadn't realized that we were both carrying pain and sorrow from our past and that we'd both felt so confused and unloved.

Mom had been stressed a lot, and I think that we'd both learned to downplay things so that we didn't make more trouble. We'd also both learned that we had to try and do things to please her, and not just to be ourselves.

After a long moment, during which I recalled her sweet, wide face framed with pale brown hair, her wide smile and ready laugh, I was able to say something.

"Thanks, Teagan," I said.

"What for?"

"For being ready to talk about this stuff. I think we both needed that."

"Yeah," he agreed, grinning. "I think so too. It's amazing how much stuff a person can carry from their past...it's so important to talk more."

"Yeah."

We both sat quietly for a long while. I finished my bowl of curry and took some more bread.

"I wanted to ask you something," I said shyly. I felt more able to trust Teagan now that we had talked about the past. "I've wanted to ask you for ages, actually."

"Yeah, sure," my brother said, leaning forward over the table. His brown eyes were soft. "I'd be happy to answer anything."

"Great. I wanted to ask you about that girl I dated. At my work, you know? I have been wondering if maybe she did feel pressured by me." I felt my throat tighten, just thinking it. I felt so ashamed. "I don't know how to tell, and I feel ashamed that it never even occurred to me before." I took a breath, sure my worry showed on my face.

"No," Teagan said instantly.

"No?"

"Brett, you know..." He began carefully. "I spoke suddenly when I said that about her feeling threatened. And I misjudged you. Sure, a lot of people would just take advantage and not really think about it – especially if they were too self-absorbed to look too carefully at how the other person responded. But I had no reason to think you might be like that. I think you would notice something like that."

I let out a deep breath. "You do?" I wasn't too sure myself anymore. I could almost believe that Christina had not really wanted me, that she had tolerated me and then suddenly not been able to tolerate any more. She was so hard to read! She never really talked about anything; her real feelings hidden behind a big wall inside.

"Yes. I really think that. But, you know," he added after a long moment. "I think that my opinion doesn't count here. The only person you should really ask is her."

"What?" I stared. I felt choked by nerves. "No. Bro, I feel a lot for her but I couldn't ask her that. I guess I just don't have the nerve." I felt ashamed about it, but I had to tell him because that was true. I didn't think I could call Christina and ask her what she really thought of me.

I couldn't really understand the look in those soft brown eyes. It could have been pity, but it felt warmer and heartfelt and I looked back, trying to understand what he meant. After a moment, he cleared his throat.

"You know, you really shouldn't doubt yourself so much. I am sure she really wants you. Why wouldn't she? You're handsome, funny, kind...you're a great guy. I think nobody could fail to see that."

I cleared my throat. "Yeah. But with the money, I can never really tell if all anybody sees when they see me is a big bank cheque." I let out a breath, feeling really tired. The topic of people not seeing me, just seeing the cash, upset me.

Teagan chuckled. "Well, maybe some people would see that. But they'd have to be so shallow they could slide out of the elevator doors. I am sure that you wouldn't be friends with such people."

"Thanks," I said. "And thanks for talking this evening...it's been great."

"Thank you, too," he said.

We finished our meal, both lost in our own thoughts. I found my mind wandering to Christina again and again, wondering how she was and what she really thought. I could feel worried for her now, too – if she really was ill, I hoped she'd get better soon.

I decided to text her as soon as I got home and ask her if she'd see me on the weekend for a hike – it would be great to be able to talk to her about all the stuff that was on my mind and finally find out more about her.

Chapter 21: Christina

I went to bed in my own apartment that night, falling asleep heavily the instant my head hit the pillow. I woke up with sunshine filtering through the curtain onto my back, warm and reassuring and relaxing.

Dressing for work was fun, now that I had my whole wardrobe to choose from – I chose a black skirt and a nice pale mauve blouse. I couldn't help wondering what Brett would think of it

The New York traffic hit me like a wall when I drove out and into the main road. It was later than I usually got out, and I knew I was going to be stuck for ages. I was grateful for good music – at least it would give me a distraction from the seething, impatient mass around me.

I felt my heart thudding as I got near my workplace. I recalled seeing my father there and I felt my hands tighten on the steering. I was frightened that he wouldn't have given up so easily – after all, I hadn't heard from him again, and that was odd in itself. I would have felt more reassured if he had been calling me constantly, rather than turning up randomly where I least expected him.

I got out of the car and walked down to the building. I was wearing high-heeled shoes – I have always been a big fan of high-heels, since I am petite and it feels good to add an extra two inches to my height. I couldn't walk particularly fast, but I walked purposefully across the carpark, trying not to be intimidated by my fear of my father still being there.

I spotted someone watching me as I got about halfway down the carpark.

"Stop being silly," I told myself harshly. I was starting to see danger everywhere. Why would some random guy be following me?

I started walking again, doing my best to ignore him. I walked up to the edge of the carpark, and when I turned around, he'd gone.

"You see?" I told myself firmly. It was just some guy, loitering in the car-park. It wasn't a criminal offense to stand and watch people! I really was losing my grip – I should talk to somebody.

I went up and round towards the front door.

"Morning, Ms. Bradfield," the guard at the door greeted me. I smiled at him, finding his presence more than usually reassuring this morning.

"Morning, Ben," I greeted him. "Bit late this morning, aren't I?" I checked the clock on the wall in the reception area. It said nine a.m.

"Not really – it's just nine a.m. now," he said, looking down at his watch. "Have a nice day."

"Thanks, Ben. You too."

I walked up through the big stone-tiled entrance, my shoes loud across the floor. I was relieved to get inside, and even more relieved to get up to my office. Lamar, the secretary, greeted me warmly as I walked down the hallway past her desk.

"Christina! Hi! Great to see you – I hope you're feeling better." She smiled at me with genuine appreciation.

"Yeah, I'm okay," I agreed. "Thanks. It wasn't anything serious."

"Great," she said happily. "I just remembered I had some forms for you to sign. I'll bring them over as soon as you're settled."

I went back to my office, hoping to see Brett. I didn't really have an excuse to pop in to see him, but I hoped that I could think of something. I wanted to talk to him and, well, just to see him really – I already missed him, even after just a day of not being able to sit down and have a chat with him.

I looked up as Neela came into my office.

"Hey!" she greeted. Her smile was bright and genuine "How are you? So good to see you back at work."

I smiled. "It's good to be back," I said. "I have so much to catch up on, even after just one day away from here."

"I know exactly what you mean! Well, I should let you get on with it. Maybe we could have lunch? I might be a bit late...I have to finally present my new color-scheme ideas to the department." She grinned, wide-eyed. I grinned back.

"Great. And I want to see those – I am sure they are beautiful. You have real skills."

"Thanks." She made a face, but I could see she was really pleased.

At lunch, I walked down the stairs and out into the street. I was going along, navigating my way through the crowd, when somebody bumped into me. I cried out, annoyed – he had pushed me quite hard, actually – and I turned around to rebuke him, when I noticed that my handbag was gone.

"Hey!" I screamed. "Hey! Stop!"

I wasn't thinking – a wash of rage flooded through me and I ran after him. I had to get that back! I had to! I had my phone in my pocket, thankfully, and my keys, but everything else was in that bag! I ran after him, heedless of my shoes or the fact that my legs ached. I weaved through between people, running down an alley.

It was only when I lost sight of him that I realized how stupid that was. I was in an alley, without the faintest idea of where I was. It was dark and smelled like tar and damp and I felt scared, heart thudding.

"Hey!" I shouted down the road, looking around for my assailant. "Hey! I'll get the police on you if you don't come out."

I might have been shouting, but it was because I was terrified.

I knew I was in danger, and there was nothing I could do about it. I looked down the alley – the buildings were close and tall and a fetid smell hung in the air. I felt my heart thudding. I turned to walk back up the street, but somebody walked out in front of me.

"Get out of my way," I whispered. I was too scared to shout. The man standing in front of me was tall and reasonably-slim, with broad shoulders. He was wearing jeans and a nondescript shirt and had graying hair, his face thin and hard. I had never seen him in my life, but he was looking at me with intensity. Suddenly I realized where I had seen him.

"You were in the carpark," I whispered.

He didn't say anything. I knew that the best thing I could do under the circumstances was to scream. Weirdly, it was the last thing that felt natural, and I cleared my throat, drew in a breath, and did my best to shout.

Chapter 22: Brett

I was already tired, and I had only been at work for a few hours. It was mainly because I was trying to ignore my urge to go and check on Christina. I needed to know if she was back safely. It just so happened that this was a day full of things to do. I went down the hallway to go and meet with the chief financial officer.

When I passed Christina's office, I looked in. I couldn't see her in there, but a young lady walked past a moment later, carrying forms and with a bewildered expression.

"Hi," I greeted her as she slowed down. "Um, is Ms. Bradfield in?"

"Yes, I think so," she replied, looking up at me with big hazel eyes. "She came in this morning. I didn't see her come back from lunch." A frown creased her brow, visible under the fall of hair across her forehead.

"I see," I said. I looked at my watch. It was two o' clock. Maybe she was having a business lunch and forgot about the time.

I managed to get my mind off the subject of where Christina was, focusing instead on the annual budget report that needed to be finished next month. There were a lot of points to clarify. I found myself wishing Christina was here so I could talk to her – she had a keen mind and I trusted her with her concise explanations more than I did Burgess and his in-depth legal knowhow.

When the meeting was finished, I hurried down to her office again.

"Is Ms. Bradfield back?" I asked the secretary. I was trying to hide my anxiety, and I supposed my worry must have sounded like anger, because she grew instantly defensive.

"I'm sure she'll be back soon. She probably had to talk to the guys from the tax office or something...it's not like her to just take off because she feels like it."

"Maybe," I agreed, trying to sound unbothered. "Let me know when she's back, please."

The secretary nodded, but I could tell she was concerned about Christina and she still thought she was in trouble. "Yes, Mr. Caden."

I went back to my office, wondering if all my employees thought I was draconian. I didn't think I was such a horrid boss. The only person I had ever treated even remotely unfairly had been Christina, now that I thought of it – I had often picked out errors in her slides at meetings, or been a smartass at her expense. I had deliberately been horrid; but just because I was attracted to her and it was the only way I could think of to fight how I felt. I found myself tapping my fingers on the desk, a habit when I was stressed and unsettled.

I let out a sigh. I should try to calm down. The secretary was right – Christina was probably off at a meeting somewhere.

"Mr. Caden?" My own secretary said, coming into the office. "A call for you. It's the chief technical officer."

"I'll take it in here. Thanks," I nodded.

The meeting lasted longer than I had expected, and by four o' clock I was glad to finally see the chief technical officer out of my room. I wanted to call Christina.

I shut the door and sat down, taking out my phone. I was surprised that I felt nervous. I suppose that I couldn't quite ignore the idea that she was mad at me. After all, it was a distinct possibility – I hadn't heard from her since Sunday, apart from a terse note to say she was fine, with no explanation given.

I dialed and waited. The phone rang and then was abruptly silent. "Weird."

I put it down, leaning back in my chair. I tried to figure out what had happened.

This wasn't like Christina. If she had been sick, she would have stayed at home again, not come in and then left after half a day. Not unless she had suddenly relapsed. In which case, how ill was she? I spontaneously decided to go and find her.

"I have to go out, on urgent personal business," I told my secretary. "Please forward important calls."

"Yes, sir."

I could remember very well where her apartment was, and I swung into the carpark after half an hour in heavy traffic and jumped out, ringing the doorbell.

"Christina? Hello?"

No reply.

I was really feeling frantic. I should have done something yesterday when she was off work! I should have come to visit her, or called. But, then, she'd seemed fine when I texted – her reply had been terse, but I had been so preoccupied with thinking that it was my fault to consider what was happening to her.

I didn't know anything, so I went back to my car. I called Teagan. I explained that Christina was missing.

"I see. Have you gone past her house?" He asked.

"I'm at her house," I said. I felt my heart thudding in my chest. "I really am a bit stressed. I can't imagine what could have happened."

I could hear my brother was worried too when he replied. "She isn't at home and she isn't at work. Do you know where else she might have gone? Does she have family here?"

"I don't know!" I almost shouted. I was really worried. "I don't think so. She wasn't born here. Sorry," I added. I tried to calm down. I knew so little about Christina, and that was my fault. I didn't even know if she had relatives here.

"I know. You're stressed," he said gently. "I can hear that. Would you like to come over? Maybe we can figure this out together."

I felt myself relax at the thought of going over. "Yes. That'd really help."

"Great. See you soon. I'll get something cooking in the meanwhile – you can't think properly on an empty stomach."

"Thanks."

I drove to my brother's apartment. The drive took over half an hour. I jumped out of the car and rang the bell, feeling a sense of urgency I couldn't explain. I needed to get to Christina.

My brother let me in and I went straight through to the sitting-room. I couldn't sit still, though, and ended up walking to the window and back, my legs not letting my body rest. I felt better walking. I told my brother what I knew as I went from the window and back.

"She switched off when I called her the first time. The second time she just let it ring."

"How likely is it," my brother asked slowly, "that she's in danger..? I mean, if we think about it logically. Is there anyone who would threaten her?"

"Who would want to threaten her?" I demanded. "She's my finance executive, not a CIA agent." I knew I was being mean, but I was just scared. I looked across at my brother but he looked perfectly calm.

"Why don't we call again?" Teagan asked. "I can see you're really worried. I know a guy who was in the police-force. He could get a trace on her number. At least then we'll know where she is."

I felt a flicker of joy in my heart. "You can do that? Sounds great," I said. "But maybe let's hold on for a bit. I'll call her again and see if she answers."

I took out my phone and pressed her number. Nothing happened. This time, the phone rang for a few seconds and then went off.

"No reply," I said.

My brother's frown deepened.

"This is pretty weird," he agreed. "If you can wait, I'll call Grayson. Maybe he can find out where she is."

I let out my breath in a long sigh. I felt so relieved!

I waited while my brother spoke to his friend. I couldn't hear much of what was being said – on Teagan's side there was mostly just nodding and agreeing.

"He'll be over shortly," he said. "Then we'll find out where she is."

"Great," I agreed.

Grayson arrived about ten minutes later – a tall, serious guy with a thin face and short gray hair, cropped to police-standard length, even though he was no longer serving as a policeman. He greeted me formally.

"Hi. I'm Matthew. You can call me Grayson, though – that's what everyone calls me."

"Hi, Grayson. I'm Brett, Teagan's brother. I'm glad to meet you. I know it sounds like I'm making a fuss about nothing, but could you trace a number for us?"

"Yeah, sure, I think so," Grayson agreed. "Can you call now?"

"Sure," I said, hastily pulling out the phone. I had suddenly got a horrible thought – what if whoever it was who kept stopping the call had decided to put the phone off? How could we trace her? I held the phone to my ear, desperate to hear something on the other side.

"It went through!" I almost shouted.

"Good. Just keep the call open, and I'll take it from here," my brother's friend said. He took the phone from me and I didn't watch what he was doing. I was too busy hoping it would work. I sat in the chair by the window, trying to look as if I wasn't completely stressed.

"Got it!"

I jumped up out of the chair as Grayson spoke. I went over to him, my heart thudding.

"Where is she?" I asked quickly.

Grayson looked at Teagan, and I tried not to shout or to demand the information. He had a worried look.

"She's in not a very nice area, actually," Grayson said worriedly. "It's down where the factories are – or where most of them were…now there are a lot of disused buildings down there and it's pretty dangerous."

"What the hell?" I was suddenly terrified for her. "Grayson! Are you sure?"

"As sure as I am that technology works," Grayson said calmly. He looked at Teagan, and I could see the police officer in him coming out again. He seemed absolutely calm, where the rest of us were really worried. "Come on. We should call the guys to go get her."

"Yes!" I agreed instantly. "We need to get the cops. But can we go too?" I asked.

Grayson shrugged, looking at me like he didn't think I would be much use. I felt offended, but at the same time I could see his point – Grayson and Teagan were both really big guys. At the same time, I wanted to be there.

"Yeah," Grayson nodded. "I reckon the guys could do with some help. And I am sure you want to be there. Come on. Let's go!"

I nodded and put my phone back in my pocket and grabbed my coat. Grayson and Teagan were talking to each other in low voices and I wondered what was worrying them. When I went back over, Grayson cleared his throat.

"I don't think my truck will take us that fast. And your brother says his car's got an issue with the rear wheel."

I grinned, taking my keys from my pocket.

"I have a BMW sports car," I said. "I reckon we'll get there on time."

My brother and Grayson looked at each other, then back at me. I nodded to them and they fell into step behind me.

My humor at their surprise was brief and lukewarm in the face of Christina's danger. I was just grateful that we would be able to get there fast.

Chapter 23: Christina

I looked around me. It was dark and I was lying on a hard floor. When my eyes got used to the light, I realized that it wasn't all that shadowed – there was faint light coming through one of the windows across the room, high above my head. I pushed myself upright, trying to see. It was cold and I fastened my blazer, grateful that I'd put it on.

"I need to get out of here."

My hands and feet were free, which was something, at least. I could remember being in the alley, and that man who'd grabbed me. I felt my heart thump. Where were they? And what had they brought me here for?

I tried to get an idea of my surroundings. I was terrified – I had no idea of when somebody would come in and how much time I had to try to get away.

I was in some sort of warehouse, I decided. It was dusty and the floor and walls were concrete, badly finished and grime-stained. The window was too high for me to climb up to, especially with nothing at all in the room to stand on. The ceiling was lost somewhere in the dark, the beams just visible in the powdery light from the window.

What could I do? I would have to find some other opening besides the window – they sure didn't get me in here through there since it was probably eighteen feet off the ground. There must be a door, but I was fairly sure it would be locked.

"Where the hell am I?" I asked myself.

I limped to the wall, still wearing my high heels. My feet were so painful I could barely walk, but I had to – I needed to find the way out of here. My eyes had got a bit better in the dark, and I could make out that the floor was pale gray, the walls dark gray. I ran my hand along the wall, feeling for a door.

I had almost found one when I heard someone talking.

"No! No, Jackson. Out of the question. No...you get that money like you said you would, or we'll kill her. Understood?"

I felt sick. Jackson was my father. He had clearly gotten himself into debt with some people who meant business. I shut my eyes. I knew perfectly well that my father had no money to speak of. He wouldn't be able to pay the debt. I wanted to scream it at them! Maybe I could pay it. I had savings. If they just wanted money, I'd give it to them just to get free.

"No! You're the one who told us where she lived. You're the one who said you could get the cash. Now, you have forty-eight hours or she's dead."

I threw up. I crouched on my knees, my stomach heaving. My father had told them where I lived!

The door opened as I struggled to my feet. I wiped my mouth and pressed my body flat to the wall.

Someone stepped into the room. I heard their feet cross towards where I had been lying, and then someone shouted.

"Where is she?"

I stayed where I was, flattened against the wall. I was close to the door. If I dropped to my knees, I could maybe crawl through before they spotted me.

"Hey! She's here!" someone shouted. "Don't let her get out of the door!"

I stood up, ready to run, but someone slammed the door shut from the other side and the man who was now in the room with me ran towards me. I screamed, more with rage than fear, falling on him and kicking and hitting, letting out all my fury and terror in a reaction so visceral that I didn't have to think. I wasn't thinking, or I would never attack anyone.

"Hey!" the man shouted, and I felt someone grip my shoulders, shaking me. His arms were so strong that I couldn't fight back and I felt my response change from fighting, or fleeing, to just going rigid.

I felt the man's hands tighten on my shoulders and he glared at me. I shut my eyes – I was not going to look at that expression. It was terrifying to me. I held my breath and I wasn't particularly inclined to praying, but I did.

All I wanted was to get out of here.

I felt him let go of me. I opened my eyes and put my hands out as I slipped and fell on the floor, unbalanced.

"You're as wily as Jackson," he spat. "I told the guys to tie you up, but no...they're too smart for that." He stepped across the floor, and I struggled to my feet again, desperate to not be too helpless in front of him. My heart was racing, I felt sick and I was numb with fear.

"Please," I whispered. "Let me go. I can pay, if it's money you need. You don't need to do anything to me."

He sniffed. "You got six hundred thousand stacked up somewhere?"

I felt my mouth open. "Six hundred thousand? No way!" I stared at him in horror. "Nobody has that kind of money saved up." Nobody except perhaps for Brett Caden, but I wasn't going to mention him. My heart ached at the thought of him. I wanted to see him again! I suddenly remembered I had my phone in my pocket. I reached my hand in to feel if it was still there. It was.

It was the one chance I had.

He laughed. "Yeah. That's what we thought," he said. "But we need that cash. Your father owes us. And if we don't get it..."

"Please," I whispered. "Please. You can't kill people for money."

"People I know were killed for less than you would be. That's how it works."

I shut my eyes, leaning back on the wall. I didn't believe in a world like that. In my world, people weren't killed for money. But then, my world wasn't a warehouse in the middle of nowhere, and I didn't know how I was going to get out of here and back to somewhere that made any sort of sense.

"Please," I whispered.

He spat on the floor. I could see rage in his body – in the set of his legs, the way he held his arms at his sides. I knew why, too. He didn't really want to kill me either. He was trying to work himself up to it. He just glared at me and went to the door.

"If you try and get out again, we're going to tie you up," he said.

I didn't say anything; just stepped away from where I leaned against the wall. I was so tired. Nothing made sense anymore. I was floating in my mind, my brain drifting, cut off from everything around me. I waited for him to go out and I heard a key grate in the door.

I rolled up on the floor, and weirdly my mind went to Brett and I wished he was here. I wished I could see him again.

Chapter 24: Brett

I clung to the wheel, driving madly down the road. "How long have we been driving for?" I asked.

"Half an hour," Grayson said from where he sat in the back. He still had my phone and some equipment with him – the coordinates of Christina's whereabouts. "And if the cops get you for speeding, we might have some explaining to do."

"You can't expect me to go slowly!" I shouted.

Beside me, Teagan tried to be rational. "We aren't going that much over the limit, Grayson," he said. "And it's not like there are going to be traffic police this far out of town."

"Probably not," Grayson agreed. "But you can't be too careful."

"Depends what you mean by careful."

I was trying to make myself angry. Actually, I was terrified. The neighborhood we were in was easily the roughest place I'd ever seen – a rickety road, buildings in various stages of disrepair and spray-paint splattering the once-white walls. I felt sick.

Christina was here somewhere.

"Where are we?" I called to Grayson, who was still watching the navigational device.

"We're close. Turn right here. Where the hell are the cops?" he complained. "I called them half an hour ago."

"They've got to get here soon," I said, trying to convince myself. I was sure they were doing their best, but with the best will in the world they couldn't get here any faster. I was just glad we'd come too.

"Yeah, I'm sure they can," Grayson agreed. "Okay. Now, we're very close. It's at the end of this street. I think we should stop the car and get out now. We don't want to alert them. And maybe we should wait until the cops get here. Is anyone armed?"

I shook my head. Teagan gestured at the trunk. "I have a firearm in that bag I brought with me. Yes, it's licensed, before anyone asks. I only have it for when I go on long hikes."

"Hell." I grinned at my brother. "I didn't even know you could shoot."

"Uncle Dean. He taught me one summer holiday."

"Oh." I was surprised, but we didn't have any time to spare talking about who could shoot and who couldn't. Grayson took the gun and we walked up the road together. My shoes crunched on gravel. My stomach was clenched with the kind of fear I couldn't even begin to describe. It was the most frightening and urgent situation I had experienced by a long way.

We walked down a narrow street between two warehouses. The surface of the road was bumpy and uneven and I could see potholes everywhere. I was not at all surprised that the factories here had been abandoned – nobody would be able to drive down this road and the whole area had a neglected, dirty feel.

"There it is," Grayson said. He'd put the tracking stuff somewhere, and he had his hand in his pocket where the gun was. He was pointing down the road towards a warehouse on our left. Teagan looked across at him and cleared his throat.

"Grayson," he said. "I know you're an ex-policeman. But we are laypeople and have no idea what we're doing and no experience. Personally, I think we should wait."

I nodded. "If we do something dumb, then we're just going to put her in more danger. I don't think we should move until the actual police get here – I totally agree. No disrespect to you, Grayson, but we have no idea what we're doing. I don't want to risk Christina."

Grayson cleared his throat. I didn't know what he was going to say – whether he agreed or disagreed with us. We didn't get any chance to find out, because as he cleared his throat, a gun fired somewhere.

I felt my heart stop.

"We have to do something," I said. I felt sick. That was...

I didn't even complete the thought. I wasn't going to let myself even entertain the idea that someone had shot Christina. But we had to do something.

"Let's go," I said.

I felt Teagan's hand on my shoulder as I strode forward.

"Let's just make a plan, quickly." he said.

"Okay," I said. I looked at Grayson. He took a deep breath. I was glad to have him with us – at least somebody here knew what they were up to. He cleared his throat and started to talk.

"Now, I reckon we should split up. Who wants to go around the back? I'll go round the front. Seeing as I have the only gun, I should face these guys. You can whistle for me if you go in."

"Great," I nodded.

"Should we go round the back?"

"Yes."

I went with Teagan, who led us between a stack of containers and a tall, white wall sprayed with colorful images and rude slogans. We didn't have time to look around – my mind was focused on Christina, who was somewhere around here. My heart was racing and I was consumed by the need to get in there and get to her before something happened.

We came out behind the warehouse. I followed Teagan out towards it, then froze as I spotted someone around the back. I could see him outside the big door, and if he hadn't moved towards the doors I would never have spotted him against the jumble of boxes and crates against the buildings.

"There's someone there."

Teagan stopped dead in front of me. He peered across to the warehouse and then nodded. "Yeah. I see him. What do we do?"

I lifted one shoulder. "Wait until he goes in? Then we follow him."

My brother raised a brow, and I thought he looked impressed and nervous, but he nodded at me.

"Let's go."

Chapter 25: Christina

People were shouting somewhere. That was the first thing that seeped into my awareness. I had somehow managed to fall asleep. I was lying on the floor, curled up, my coat pulled tight around me. I was only waking up and my mind came to alertness slowly. I looked around, trying to figure out exactly where I was in the room. It was not quite pitch dark yet, the window a square of pale blue, still pouring dusky light onto the floor. I focused on what had disturbed me. Human voices, raised in fear and anger.

I listened as they came down a hallway, their voices echoing.

"What the hell? How did anyone find us?"

"I don't know! How the hell would I know?" Somebody shouted back. The two were just outside the door where I was, their booted feet coming towards me fast

I stood up. I sensed that things would not go well for me should they find me. I slid my feet out of my shoes – my toes were raw and aching from the high heels – and flattened myself against the wall.

"Get her out of here," the first man to speak was shouting. I could hear his voice through the door, and the urgency in his tone made me sweat with fright. The door swung open.

"What should we do with her?" the second man demanded.

"What do you think? We need to get that money. Get hold of her father! Tell her father he has two hours."

Two hours. No! I felt my heart almost stop beating. What was I going to do? I had two hours before somebody shot me.

I held my breath and shut my eyes, trying to disappear into the dark.

"Where the hell is she?" the second voice shouted. A flashlight beam – bright and harsh – washed across the space where, a few minutes ago, I had been lying fast asleep.

"How should I know?" the first man demanded. "Do you think she climbed through that window?" He laughed.

"No," the second man said, sounding embarrassed.

"Well! Find her! Look, give me that flashlight."

I heard a brief struggle, during which I tried to edge towards the door. If I could just get through, they wouldn't be able to catch me.

"There she is! Who the hell left the door open!"

"Run! After her!"

I ran down the hallway. My feet hurt and every step was agonizing, but I didn't have time to stop and think about it. I ran, screaming, to the end of the hallway. There was a door there and I burst through, raw terror making me scream again as I stopped. I was surrounded by people.

"Help!" I screamed. "Please! Help!"

The men in the room looked astonished and then one of them grabbed at me.

"How the hell did you get here? Who let you out? Shut her up, for crying out loud!" a man shouted at me. I waited for somebody to grab me; my body frozen to the spot with fear. But all of the men in the room had frozen too, listening to something.

At that moment, I heard footsteps in the corridor. I thought that my attackers from the other room had caught up with me, but then I looked up to see a big gray-haired man and another brown-haired guy with huge shoulders. They were standing in the doorway and one of them had a gun.

"Get your hands up!" he demanded. "All of you!"

I felt a flood of relief, and then my eyes fixed on another face that had appeared in the doorway. This face was long and slim and had big brown eyes that stared into mine, full of love and tenderness. He held out a hand to me. It was Brett Caden.

"Brett!" I shouted. I felt tears running down my cheeks. He was here! He'd come to save me! I had never imagined, in my wildest dreams, that would happen!

"Christina," he said. He dropped to his knees, taking my hand. "Let's get out of here."

"Brett," I said. I couldn't think of anything else to say. My tears were running down my cheeks, my heart aching with relief and happiness. All around us, people were shouting and swearing, and I could hear the gray-haired man trying to keep order, his gun still pointing at the three men in the room.

"Let's get out of here," he said.

I took his hand and we ran down the hallway together, just as a gun went off. I screamed, and Brett held me and we ran, blindly, down the hallway and then to the right and then, as we burst out into the cool air, I heard something I had not been expecting to hear. Police cars.

Blue lights flashed, and the sirens were loud and Brett held me against him, my face buried in his chest as he stroked my hair and held me tight.

"It's okay," he said softly, his words gentle as he repeated them, over and over. "It's okay, we're safe."

I was crying, my poor body exhausted and my mind confused and afraid. What was happening to those men? Who were they? They had clearly come with Brett to save me, and now they were also in danger.

"The others," I whispered.

"They're okay," he said gently, though I could see worry in his eyes too. "They're coming out now."

I let out a sigh of relief, then cried out joyfully as the two big men came out of the warehouse. I could see them in the light from the police cars, their shoulders slumped, their faces strained. One of the men had a hand pressed tight to his shoulder and I gasped, then Brett and I were walking over to join them.

"Hey, guys. What happened?" Brett asked gently.

"The police are in there now. One guy let off a round, but nobody got badly hit," the dark-haired man said. He smiled at me. "Hey," he greeted. "I'm Teagan."

"Hi," I said, turning to frown up at Brett.

"He's my older brother," Brett said.

I stared. Now that I knew, I could see a faint resemblance between the two – they both had brown eyes and glossy brown hair, but Teagan's face was broad and homely, though he had the same shaped eyes as his brother, and when he smiled the grin was similar.

"I'm pleased to meet you. Christina Bradfield."

"This is Matthew. Grayson, as he likes to be called. He's been shot, but it's not serious."

"Oh!" I gasped. "Oh, good," I added, as Mr. Grayson held out a hand – the other was still pressed firmly to his shoulder.

"Good to meet you, Ms. Bradfield."

I shook his hand, and Brett gently turned Mr. Grayson to face the police-cars. "Grayson, you need someone to see to that arm," he said.

"Not...bad," Grayson said, but I could see his teeth were gritted and that it had taken all of his energy to greet me. Brett and I walked with him to the police-cars, where a police officer greeted us.

"Hi. Sergeant Brownlow. Are you injured, sir?"

"Yes. I am. I'm ex-captain Grayson. Got a shot in the arm. Could you have a look?"

"Sure," she said.

We left them to it. Brett walked back with me around the corner of the building. I was limping and he stopped, looking down at me worriedly.

"What happened?" He asked, his voice tight with concern. He took my hands, looking into my eyes with worry. "What happened to your leg?"

"Nothing," I said. "My feet...they're really painful, and I can't..."

"Christina!" he gasped, his voice full of love and frustration. "You have no shoes! Come on. Let's get you back to the car. The others will join us. You need to get to a doctor."

"I'm fine, Brett," I said softly. "Really. All I want is to get home."

"Okay," he said tenderly. He wrapped his arms around me and lifted me up, my legs over his one arm, my head resting on his other arm. I felt myself melt against him, and the whole world seemed to shrink until it consisted of just us, my head resting on his shoulder, his arms holding me tight. I could smell the scent of him – leather and cologne. I shut my eyes and felt the faint sway and wobble as he carried me across uneven ground.

"We'll just wait for the others, and then I'll take you home," he promised, setting me down on the back seat. His eyes were gentle on mine and he held my hand in his own. I felt my own eyes droop sleepily as I rested my head on the rest.

I heard him get into the front seat, and I felt suddenly so sleepy – too sleepy to even lift my head up.

A moment or two later, I woke to hear people getting into the car. The doors slammed and Brett spoke in a low voice.

"Christina's asleep in the back. Try not to wake her."

"Yes, Brett."

I tried to sit up, but I was too sleepy and I curled up on the seat, letting the slow rise and fall of the car over the bumpy road soothe me to sleep.

When I next woke, we were pulling up on the roadside. I blinked sleepily. The streetlight shone in brightly through the window and I could vaguely recognize the tall building opposite, the way the street-sign was just across from us.

"We're at my apartment?"

"Yes," Brett's voice said from close to me. He was facing me from the driver's seat, neck bent to be able to see me. His hand took mine. "I'll take you upstairs."

"Where is Teagan?" I asked.

Brett smiled. "I dropped him off at his home. Grayson's gone to get his wound checked, but I reckon he'll be fine. He was very much okay."

"Good," I said. I was so sleepy! I woke as Brett got out and opened my door, reaching to lift me up.

"I can walk," I whispered faintly.

"No, you can't, Miss Bradfield," he said gently. "I am going to carry you upstairs now."

I didn't argue, just lay in his arms as he shut the door and carried me across towards the apartment block. Luckily, my keys were in my blazer pocket and I passed them to him. He unlocked the door and carried me into the lift. I kept my eyes shut. The bright light stung and I buried my face in his shoulder.

I opened my eyes as Brett put me down, very gently, on the couch. He bent down and kissed my cheek, my heart melting at the tenderness of it.

"I'm going to get some bandages for your feet," he said. "You are sure you're okay?" His eyes scanned mine worriedly and I held his hand between mine.

"I'm fine," I assured him. I knew he was worried that somebody had hurt me.

"Okay," he said. "I'll go and get those bandages."

"In the cabinet..." I murmured, hearing his footsteps going off towards my bedroom. I woke to feel his hands on my feet, cool and soothing as he gently massaged them. My body relaxed, the tension instantly giving way to a tender relief as his touch sent a wash of feeling through my system.

"Brett, you don't have to do that," I said, grinning at him as he gently pressed my feet, relaxing the pain and bruises from their aching toes.

"Shh," he said, and grinned back. "Let me take care of you. I know you like being in charge, but just relax and let me help for once."

I smiled and felt all the fear and worry inside me melt into warm, intense feelings and a sudden longing to be held.

He seemed to sense it too, because he bent down and pressed his lips to my forehead and gently lifted me and carried me to my bedroom.

Chapter 26: Christina

I rolled over sleepily as Brett slipped in under the covers. I was so tired, but the moment I felt his arm around me, his touch gentle on my hair, I felt my body flood with fresh strength.

"Hello there," he whispered, his chin resting on my shoulder, his hand on my arm.

"Hello."

I turned around, my body pressed to his, my lips seeking his as he held me close. I could feel his hard chest under my breasts, his body muscled and his arms tight around me, drawing me closer still.

I felt his tongue, warm and soft, in my mouth and my body melted with longing as he drew me against him. His hands moved down my back, stroking me gently, and I pressed against him, my own hands questing down his muscular body, reaching lower to grasp him in my hand.

He gasped and I squeezed and I could hear him trying to control his breathing. I was surprised by how much I longed for him, how much I ached to feel the firm hardness in my hand elsewhere in me.

He pushed against me and then he swung to lie on top of me, looking into my eyes with a tender softness.

"Let me," he said. "I want to spoil you."

I shut my eyes, feeling his lips move on my neck, moving lower, kissing my breasts and then moving down to my belly. He parted my thighs and I cried out as his tongue found the hardness in my folds, licking and flickering over it with maddening tenderness.

I gasped and tried to hold still as he pressed more firmly, his tongue working me harder now, his fingers stroking me and making my nerves light up with uncontrollable wonderment. His warm tongue pushed against me, insistently, flicking and sucking and I could hear my breathing, shallow and urgent, as sensation rushed through me.

I cried out as I came, and he held me, his head resting on my belly as I gasped and tried to get my breath back, my mind floating in a white haze of sheer intensity.

He lay there, letting me rest, and then gently rolled over and put his knee between mine, his body pressing on mine as he looked into my eyes.

I felt him move against me, and he entered me so slowly, his thick hardness pushing into me, buried full-length, which was considerable, inside me. I lay back, fresh new fires of longing washing through my nerves as he repeated it, pulling out and plunging in, until I could take all his fullness.

I gasped and wrapped my arms around him, holding him as he moved slowly, rubbing on the special spots inside me, my nerves lighting up as he thrust and pushed inside.

I couldn't hold still now, and he must have sensed my excitement, because he started to go faster, moving and pulling out and in, out and in, with a wonderful connectedness that made it seem like his body and mine were made for one another.

I was gasping, amazed at how quickly he had got me to the point of arousal.

As I cried out, he gasped, his body collapsing on top of me. We lay there, our arms tight around each other, both of us washed away on the strength of our desire.

I held him, his face beside mine, our breaths tight and gasping as we lay there, held so warmly in each other's arms. His weight felt so good on top of me, my body relaxing under him as my mind drifted in the warm sea of sated longings.

After what felt like a long time, he rolled off me. He lay beside me, his arm around me, drawing me close against him. I moved back so that his arms were wrapped around me, holding me safely. I nestled my head on the pillow beside his and I fell instantly asleep.

The next morning, I awoke to the feeling of somebody stroking the skin of my back, slowly and tenderly. My eyes shut, I pushed back against Brett, my lips smiling as he drew me close, wrapping his arms around me. I could feel he was aroused and I was too, my body longing for his.

I rolled over to kiss him, the sunshine pouring down into the bedroom. He grinned, rolling me to lie on my side, drawing me back against him.

I gasped as he reached down to stroke between my thighs.

After we had made love, my body completely relaxed, I rolled over and kissed him and he held me tight against him, his arms warm and strong as they held me completely safe. I rested a hand on his shoulder and looked into his gentle eyes.

"It's quite late," I murmured. "Should we get up and go to work?"

"No," he said, kissing me. "Let's call in sick. We have a good reason to take a day off, I think."

I nodded. "I suppose," I said, then smiled at him. "This is going to be fun."

He laughed. "Yes, it is."

We both lay there, my body warm and relaxed against his, his arms tight around me. I smiled up at him and he opened one eye, grinning sleepily at me.

"Are you awake again?"

I giggled. "I am, I'm afraid! Much as I would like to go back to sleep again."

He smiled and stroked my back. "Shall I make some breakfast? We can eat and then get back into bed if we want. We have the whole day, after all."

I grinned. "Yes," I said, feeling my heart race with excitement. "We do."

We got out of bed and went through to make breakfast together. I only had muesli and fresh milk in the house, so we had big bowls of that. The bread had gone stale, but I toasted some anyway – I was so hungry! As we sat and ate breakfast – my mind still drifting in the bliss of lovemaking – we talked together.

"I was so glad to find you," Brett said softly. "I was so frightened for you, when we found out that you were in that warehouse!" His face was a picture of worry.

I felt my own eyes widen. "You found me?" I asked, astonished. "How did you find me?"

"Grayson actually did the work. I was so stressed when you disappeared from work that I called Teagan, my brother. He was the one who knew Grayson – he was a policeman, Grayson – and he used some equipment to track the call."

"Wow!" I was impressed. I looked across at him, my heart so full of appreciation. "You really were worried about me."

He looked at me. His brown eyes were so full of love and I could see, now, how exhausted he was, along with the full weight of how concerned he had been about me. "I can't tell you how terrified I was when I couldn't reach you," he said. "I don't know how, but somehow I knew something had happened."

I held his hand wordlessly. It healed so many years of pain to hear that somebody worried for me, that somebody wanted to protect me and help me unconditionally. That someone was so connected to me that they knew when I was in trouble, when my actions were out of the ordinary.

"Thank you for coming to get me," I said. What else could I say? My voice was tight with tears and I held him wordlessly and he held me and we sat there together, silent, the flat quiet and warm around us both.

After a long moment, I sat up and reached for the milk. "I guess we should finish breakfast," I said, pouring myself some more muesli. "I'm pretty starving; I don't know about you."

He grinned. "Absolutely!"

I could see his eyes shining and I could guess that he was thinking of how we had made love. I was also thinking of it. I ate my muesli and found my mind wandering in thoughts of the previous day.

"What happened?" I asked dreamily. "After the police arrived?"

He shrugged. "Well, you saw most of it. They arrived and arrested the guys. Apparently they've been looking for them for ages. They get up to some seriously bad stuff. One of the things they do is loan money at extortionate rates and they can be super-violent if they don't get paid. The police were glad to have a tip that led to their arrest." He leaned back in his chair and just looked relieved that he'd found me, but I felt myself shiver.

"Those guys," I explained after a long moment. "They were after me because of my father. He owed them six-hundred thousand in debt. He had a gambling addiction. He was here, trying to get money from me. That was why I was avoiding work for those days...I kept on seeing him hanging around here. He was trying to get money out of me. I was scared." I covered my face with my hands, reliving the fear of the previous week. Now that it was finally over and I was finally out of danger, I could acknowledge how awful it was.

I was crying and he stood and wrapped his arms around me, holding me close.

"Christina," he said, stroking my hair. "Christina, my sweetie. You're fine," he assured me, whispering to me where he held me against his chest. "It's alright now."

I sobbed, wrapping my arms tight around his waist, my face pressed to his firm abdomen. I held him and hugged him and felt years of shame wash out of me. After a long moment, I looked up at him, drawing in a slow breath.

"You're not ashamed?" I asked. "I mean, because I come from such a different background to you? That I grew up poor, in a horrible place, with a father I was terrified of?"

He looked at me, his eyes gentle, a tender quirk to them. "How can you think I'd be ashamed?" he asked gently. "Christina, the fact that you come from that background makes you more amazing, not less. If I'd known that you had managed to get to where you are in spite of all that, it would be even more impressive – not that it isn't already impressive, but you know what I mean." He smiled.

I stared. "You mean...you really mean you're impressed? That you don't feel like you wouldn't want to be seen with me anywhere?"

He looked at me; his turn to look shocked. "Christina! How can you say that?" he sounded almost hurt. "I would be honored to be seen with you! I'd want to be seen with you absolutely anywhere. I am so proud of you."

I started crying. Relief was so powerful that I held him close, sobbing, while he whispered nonsense in my ear and held me tight. I sat back, sniffing, feeling washed clean.

"Whew. I guess this is just all so different to what I expected," I said. I wiped my nose with my hand and looked up at him, eyes damp. "I really thought that you'd hate me for that."

"For coming from a different background?" He sounded shocked. "Christina! I hope I don't look so shallow to you?"

I grinned, feeling my mouth lift at the corners. "No," I admitted. "No, Brett...you look anything but shallow. I'm sorry. It wasn't because I thought you would be like that – I thought all people would be like that. I lived with that shame my whole life. I was used to the idea that people would not like me for who I was."

"Christina," Brett said, and bent down to look into my eyes. I felt his gaze on mine. "I love you," he said. "Yes, I know that seems sudden, but I have been around for long enough to recognize it. I love you – gentle, sweet Christina. I have loved you for an awfully long time, but I've only just come to realize it. I hope that you don't mind too much if I hang around here." He ended shakily, a big grin stretching his lips.

I stared at him. I felt my heart flood with warmth. I had never expected to hear that! I knew I was in love with him. I had realized it a long while ago, I thought, but I had never thought I'd have a chance to say it. I loved him from the moment he had held me when I cried, when he had looked at me so tenderly.

"Brett," I said gently. "I love you too. I think I have known it for a while. I just couldn't bring myself to believe that it was possible, that you could love me too." I chuckled, feeling my heart melt and wetness run down my cheeks, unable to hold back tears of joy. "I love you so much, and I would be more than delighted if you hung around here for as long as you want. If you please. Provided that's a very long time indeed."

We looked at each other. He grinned at me and I grinned back and I felt my heart fill with warmth.

"Well," he said. "I think that's certainly something to look forward to."

I grinned, happy laughter bubbling up inside me as I pressed my lips to his and held him close and we kissed. I loved him so much, I realized, and I knew that I would only come to love him more. And we were safe and happy, both joyful to be sitting here, holding hands, on a warm and tranquil morning.

Epilogue:

I looked out of the window, feeling a shiver of excitement. It was evening, the lights just switched on in the cars, the dusk soft and pink over the busy, blinking city. I turned around as Brett came out of the bathroom. We were in my apartment, the view over the city wide and bright.

"Christina," he said, smiling at me. "Are you ready?"

I nodded. "Yes," I said. My hands could feel the silky fabric of my summer dress, the collar a wide boat-neck, the skirt soft and smooth and decorated with a design of purple flowers.

"You look gorgeous," Brett murmured. "I think I've never seen you in a dress before."

I chuckled. "I'm not sure if that makes me look gorgeous, or just unusual," I teased, but his brown eyes were wide and glinting with arousal. I knew that he meant I looked good.

"Christina, you look so lovely. I don't know how I'm going to keep my hands off you, but I don't want to spoil your makeup."

I giggled. "Brett! You are sweet. And I have to admit, you look gorgeous, too." I wrapped my arms around him, running my hands down his back. He was wearing a black suit, the jacket fitting perfectly across his broad shoulders, the white shirt so sexy and just begging to be unbuttoned, I thought with a delighted grin. I kissed him, then put on more lipstick as he wiped his mouth, grinning at me.

"I reckon we should go now," he said after a moment, looking at the clock. "It's about six o'clock."

"Yeah," I nodded, feeling my heart lift with excitement. "Let's go! We'll get there in plenty of time, I think."

He nodded and kissed me, but tried not to kiss off my lipstick again.

We went down to his car, both laughing and breathless. I was so excited and I could tell he was too. I wondered if he – like me – was also nervous. I couldn't help feeling a bit apprehensive – after all, this was the first time we were going to make an appearance together at work.

We drove through the streets, which were still crowded with evening traffic. I looked out at the cars, at buildings with neon signs, at the traffic-lights ahead, and felt so completely happy. It was as if when I was with him the world was another place. I smiled happily, just too full of joy to keep myself from grinning.

We arrived at the big high-rise building after a half hour's drive and we parked in Brett's parking-place. He helped me out of the car and we went up to the reception area together. I held his hand, my heart thudding. My hand tightened in his, my heart racing.

"I'm sure they'll be very happy to see us," Brett murmured.

I nodded, swallowing. "I suppose."

We smiled at each other. He also looked nervous, but he was trying to look calm. I loved him for that, just as I loved him for everything about him.

We stepped out of the lift.

I looked at the crowd. We were facing everybody from work, and a lot of investors besides. They were dressed in black suits or bright dresses, the smell of wine and perfume strong around them. I gripped Brett's hand, feeling my body tense with nerves. They were all looking at us; a wall of eyes and designer suits and I could feel myself wanting to just walk away.

Then, suddenly, Neela stepped to the front of the group. "Christina!" she greeted. "Hey! So great to see you! Hey, Mr. Caden. So good to see you here."

I relaxed instantly as some other people nodded, and some smiled. Somebody else came over to talk to Brett, while Neela talked to me. She was tall in heels, with wide trousers and a beautiful sparkly top. Her long hair was styled in a relaxed chignon and she had crystal earrings that blinked in the lights. Her eyes were even brighter as she grinned at me.

"Christina! You look amazing! So good to see you here! And that dress is stunning..." She looked across at Brett, who was talking to the CTO but glanced at both of us, a warm grin on his face.

I smiled. "I'm so happy, Neela," I said. She raised a brow, looking at Brett Caden.

"He's stunning, isn't he? So weird, I've only just noticed. I'm so happy for you, Christina. So happy."

I felt a wide smile stretch my lips. "Thank you, Neela. Really...you kept me sane when I really needed it. I'll never forget that."

She laughed. "You're very sane," she said. "I'm not sure if I can say the same for myself...come and look at the new font for our logo and you'll be able to judge for yourself."

I laughed and embraced her fondly. "You know what I mean," I teased gently.

She nodded. "I'm so glad you're okay. And that you're so happy." She gestured at Brett, who was deep in discussion with two shareholders, not looking round for a moment.

"I am. I never thought I'd find someone so wonderful, someone who understands everything about me." I watched him where he stood, his back straight, his hair soft in the light from the overhead lighting.

"He seems to be a really nice guy," Neela agreed, though she sounded so surprised that I giggled.

"Yes, he really is," I replied after a moment. "He's a wonderful man. He's accepting and understanding and supportive..." I trailed off, seeing her grin deepen.

"You really are happy," she said.

"Yes," I agreed. "So happy."

We talked a bit about her work, and gradually the conversation drifted around to the topic of my father. I hadn't spoken to him since he had turned up and tried to convince me to pay his debts. After all, he had very nearly gotten me killed, and on top of all the trouble in the past I didn't really feel like trying to be vulnerable with him. I held no hatred for him, but I couldn't feel safe around him. Since he was now let off the hook with his debt, he had agreed to try and treat his gambling addiction, and Brett had organized for him to attend a rehabilitation run by a doctor with a huge success rate. We both had every hope that he would receive the help he needed.

Other than that, I felt free of the burden. I also felt free of the terror that had been lurking in my heart for years. I was starting to heal, helped by the gentle love that I received from Brett.

Slowly, I was discovering that love was unconditional, and that I didn't need to deserve it. That Brett and I loved each other and it was a gentle, beautiful thing that we shared.

I was talking to Neela when Brett came over, just finishing with the investors. He grinned at me, shook Neela's hand when I introduced him, and stayed to chat for a bit.

"She's nice," he said when she'd left. "I'm glad you have such a good friend."

"She's a wonderful friend," I agreed warmly. "And she's your head graphic designer."

"It's great," he agreed. We both drifted over to the big posters where Neela's latest work was displayed – not only had she designed them overall, she'd done the layout for each one. We read through them, nodding admiringly at her work.

"Shall we go outside?" Brett asked, gesturing at the reception-area in general. "It's pretty warm, when so many people are packed in."

"Yes," I agreed. I reached for my jacket and shrugged it on; a soft cream-colored blazer that matched the dress exactly, as if it had been bought together. We went out onto the terrace.

"It's a beautiful evening," Brett said, coming to lean beside me on the rail.

I nodded. The city was stretched out below us, the car lights bright in the grayish dusk. I could hear the distant noise, but it didn't disturb me. I was too busy taking Brett's hand in mine, feeling the soft warmth of his fingers as they held onto mine.

"I'm so glad to be here," Brett said. His fingers tightened on mine; his expression soft. "I mean, here with you. I guess it took me a long time to realize that we both feel the way we do, but I finally got it." He chuckled. His body leaned against mine, warm and firm, and I rested my head on his shoulder.

We stood looking out over the city.

After a long moment, enjoying the silence, I turned to face him. I looked into his eyes, and my heart raced at the softness and care I saw in them. I smiled, unable to conceal how much I felt or how deeply I cared about him.

"I love you," he said softly, reaching forward, his hand cool on my face as he gently cupped it with a palm. "I am so glad to be here with you, dearest Christina."

"I love you too," I said, bending forward and kissing him, feeling those warm, firm lips part under mine, my heart racing as he drew me into his arms, his body warm and firm as he pulled me close. "I love you so much, dearest Brett. I couldn't be happier."

We kissed.

*****

Also by Erica Frost

Seduced By A Billionaire
Dark Secrets
A Billionaire's Game
Power Play
Ruthless Rival
Taming The Billionaire
The Hated Billionaire
3-Pointer